I0531111

Julie:
The Redemption Of The Backyard Bully

a novel

Rachael McIntire

ISBN 978-0615885025

Visit elishapress.com for a free digital
version of this book and other titles.

Cover illustration by Jennie McIntire. Interior
illustrations by Tim and Jennie McIntire.

Table of Contents

1

The Saturday Only Club

Grandma Greene was not really a grandma. She had never been married, but found herself being referred to in this affectionate fashion by the toddlers to tweens for whom she provided weekly watch-care. One of them was at her elbow just now, watching with eager anticipation as Grandma removed a pan of chocolate chip cookies from the oven. Since Grandma had let her help mix some of the ingredients, little Emily felt she had a vested interest in the outcome.

Just as the last cookie sheet emerged from the hot oven, the kitchen lights flickered, then cut off completely, leaving Grandma and Emily in the semi-darkness of an increasingly cloudy Saturday afternoon. Grandma, ever at the ready, reached into the kitchen drawer and pulled out an old-fashioned metal flashlight. Handing it to Emily, she followed carefully while the child lit the path to the back door.

Once the door was opened, Grandma rang the old school bell for the rest of the kids to come in from play. Even with her cataracts, Grandma could see ominous clouds in the north headed their way, and with visions of five splashing pairs of muddy sneakers invading her living space, she motioned the group to race the raindrops already spotting the porch.

Warm cookies and cold milk eased the disappointment of the children, who now wondered

how they would spend the remaining hours of the
Saturday Only Club inside the four walls of
Grandma's house. Grandma had all kinds of activities
available to them on any given Saturday, but with the
electricity on the blink, there was little to do.

The motley group plopped themselves down on
the huge sofa and overstuffed chairs, or else directly
on the oval rug in front of the blazing stone fireplace,
each member of the group still without a clue as to
how they could survive the afternoon sans electricity.

Sounds of a more threatening storm than the
showers the weatherman had predicted began a
relentless rhythm against the windowpanes on the
north side of the house. Suddenly, the children were
more alarmed than bored, as huge bolts of lightning
fully illuminated the darkened living-room.

At sixty-five, Grandma Greene was a veteran of
many such storms. The calm in her voice, assuring the
children that all would be well, seemed to dissipate
their anxiety somewhat. Besides. they knew that
Grandma was well acquainted with the Creator of
storms. In her own words, He just happened to be her
Father.

Folding her apron across a kitchen chair, she
ambled into the living room to join the children
gathered there. She scooped up Donnie, a three-year-
old and currently the youngest club member, and then
plopped her tired bones into the rocking chair next to
the fireplace. Scooting unashamedly closer toward the
watchful eye of Grandma were the next youngest
children, the seven-year-old twins, Phoebe and Peter.

Shy Tommy's widening pupils betrayed his own desire to join the younger ones at Grandma's side, but at nine, he felt an unspoken restraint to appear brave. Liza, twelve, and in her estimation, NOT in need of a baby-sitter, glued herself to the far corner of the couch, determined not to display any such childish weakness.

Grandma's eyes rested protectively on each of the children in her care. If she had heard her Lord speak audibly, she could not have been more convinced that now was the time to tell the children a story – her story, and yet *His*. Her last glance before commencing this narration was toward ten-year-old Emily, whose background as an adopted child mirrored that of someone special from her own past.

"Everybody comfy?" Grandma asked. "Because the story I have to tell you may outlast the storm outside, and I want to be sure you've chosen your favorite seat." No one moved a muscle except Donnie, who nestled even closer to the narrator than before.

All the kids (even Liza) loved Grandma's stories, and with firelight as their only visual focus in the approaching darkness, a good story seemed the answer to their dilemma as well as to their unspoken fears.

2

Julie, The Schoolyard Bully

"Remember this summer," Grandma began, "when the heat wave lasted two weeks, and we had story time on Saturdays after lunch?"

Four "yeses" and a "no ma'am" (from Tommy) echoed within the group.

"You told us the story of the backyard bully," added Emily with immediate recall.

"Ooooh, she was T-E-R-R-I-B-L-E!" interjected Phoebe, pleased with her spelling prowess. Peter rolled his eyes at his kooky twin.

"Well, that particular story has a great deal more to it and it happens to be true," continued Grandma. "I know because I was there." Five pairs of ears perked up immediately with anticipation. One pair of ears, Donnie's, were sleepily giving way to the lulling rhythm of the rocking chair.

"I guess before we get into the part that you haven't heard, we should catch Tommy up on what he missed those two weeks he spent at Christian camp. Would one of you like to tell Tommy the basic facts from the story of Julie and the Gladstones?"

"I'll try," volunteered Emily, "but I may need some help. If I miss any details, could the rest of the children help me out?"

"I think that would be just fine," agreed Grandma, as she sat back in her chair to rock little Donnie.

"Well," Emily began, "first of all, I didn't know that the story Grandma told us about Julie was true. That makes it even more interesting.

"Now what we know so far is that Julie lived next door to a family by the name of Gladstone. They had a little girl named Rebecca. Shortly after the Gladstones had moved into Julie's neighborhood, somebody put a basket on their porch with a baby in it. Julie didn't know the details of the story at that time, only that the Gladstones adopted that little girl in the basket and called her Sarah.

"Julie used to tease Sarah about being born in a basket, until one day Sarah turned around and said to her, 'I'm a miracle of Jesus, you know.' When Julie heard that, she decided her mother must be right about 'those crazy Christians next door.' So she decided not to bring up the basket thing again. She couldn't think of anything else to say, anyway.

"After that, Julie just watched Sarah and Rebecca from a distance. She noticed that they always seemed happy with just a few toys. She also noticed that their parents would come out and give them rides in the tire swing or play with them in their little pool. Julie's mom and dad never did anything like that, and it made her jealous.

"One winter when Julie was twelve years old, there was a heavy snow. After it melted a little, the Gladstone girls went sledding with their new sled. They had a nice yard for that, but on Julie's side of the fence, there were too many trees.

"Julie's dad was on the road as a salesman. Her mother worked too, but this was her day off. But the store called her, and she didn't have time to get the babysitter. She made Julie promise to stay in the house, and left.

"As soon as her mom's car was out of sight, Julie decided to go out and see what the Gladstones were up to. She could hear them laughing even through the closed windows. So she put on her jacket and boots and went down the hill, pretending to look at the frozen creek, but watching the girls out of the corner of her eye. They were watching her too, afraid of her getting too close to the thin ice.

"When she got to the edge of the creek, Julie decided to do some showing off, and hopefully make her neighbors jealous of *her* for a change. She told them they were sticks in the mud, and other bad things. They were only worried about her, though, and tried to warn her to stay off the creek. But Julie just ignored them and yelled 'Watch me!' Then she stepped out on the ice and started sliding across on her boots.

"But the ice broke, and Julie went through into the water. It was very deep, and Julie couldn't swim. She would have drowned right then, only Sarah and Rebecca ran for their mother, and the three of them managed to pull Julie out of the water. Then they took her in the house and gave her warm clothes and took care of her, even though she'd been so mean to them. She was different after that.

"I guess that's the story in a nutshell, isn't it, Grandma?"

"What did you do, memorize it?" interjected Liza, a little disappointed that Emily had not forgotten a single major detail, leaving her nothing to add.

Ignoring Liza's snide remark, Grandma answered, "Great job, Emily. I couldn't have told it better myself, and I know the whole story. I decided that some day I would tell you all the rest of the story, and this seems to be the right time, especially since Tommy is with us too.

"And what you said about Julie a few minutes ago, Phoebe, was right on the mark," Grandma added. "Julie was a *very bad* little girl. Her parents had tried everything – well, almost everything – to get her to behave, but nothing seemed to change her attitude."

Maybe the fact that her dad was away from home much of the time as a salesman, or the fact that her mother had to work to make ends meet, contributed to Julie's problems. But when you get down to it, Julie, like many children, made the wrong choices in her life from a very young age. Julie was jealous.

Thrust into preschool from the age of three, Julie spent all her time focused on what everybody else had. If her current playmate had something she didn't, Julie grabbed it from her, or from him for that matter. At times she met with a little resistance, but a well-placed

shove usually sent the other child teetering backward
to the ground, or running tearfully to the teacher on
duty.

When the supervising teacher would arrive on the
scene, the item in question would be nowhere near
Julie, who would be *innocently* gathering wildflowers
from the grassy play yard. Julie managed to continue
this ploy for quite a few weeks.

One particular day, the item was a ball, and since
Scottie had brought it from home, he naturally
assumed it was his. Julie assumed the opposite, and
swung mischievously into action. Unbeknownst to
her, Mrs. Beagle, the alert principal of the preschool,
happened to be watching the children play from her
office window just as Julie knocked Scottie to the
ground.

Julie's back was to the building, and she did not
see the three-foot strides charging in her direction.
But the merry little tune she was humming to herself
suddenly changed to *uh-oh* as she heard her name
called not so sweetly, "Julie!" Taking the three-year
old firmly by the hand, Mrs Beagle quick-marched her
into the office.

Instructing Julie to sit down, Mrs Beagle took a
chair opposite, and said,"Well, Julie, if you were my
little girl, I'd warm your seat, but I'll just have to hope
your mother will take care of that little detail. For
now, we'll have to do it the hard way." Indicating
another chair in the corner of the office, Mrs. Beagle
continued, "You can sit in that chair and face the wall.
If you turn your head in the next twenty minutes, we'll

start the clock again, even if it takes all day. Do you understand?"

Julie gave Mrs. Beagle an angry nod, and climbed into the chair facing the wall. "I'll get that Scottie," she seethed, under her breath. "It's all *his* fault."

"Time out" gave Julie opportunity to think about her actions. She was sorry she had been caught, but not a bit sorry for her behavior. If this incident had happened at home, her mother would have been upset and would have threatened her with her usual "just wait till your father gets home" speech. Then, her daddy would come home – two weeks later – and all would have been forgotten. Perhaps she should steer clear of Mrs. Beagle for the present. Time-out chairs were boring.

3

Sweet Genevieve

Julie managed to get through her years in both preschool and then kindergarten without being suspended, but only because she saved her worst behavior for weekends and summer vacation. Mrs. Greene could not afford a good babysitter for her recalcitrant daughter when school was not in session, so she hired the fifty-cents-an-hour kind – teenagers.

Teenage babysitters were okay with Julie, as long as they minded their own business (t.v., telephones, and boyfriends). The neighborhood was Julie's personal turf, and at five years old, she brooked no interference.

"Hey, Joowie!" sang gentle Genevieve, the little next door neighbor. "Guess what! We're moving."

"So?" retorted Julie, trying desperately to hide her disappointment and surprise.

Rebuffed by Julie's apparent indifference to her announcement, Genevieve ducked her head with embarrassment. "Just thought you might like to know," she mumbled quietly.

Julie seldom regretted her ugly behavior, but Genevieve was the one person in the world she cared about, and she immediately did an about-face. "Aw, Genevieve, I'm sorry," she said, swallowing a huge lump of pride. "When?"

Quick to forgive, Genevieve resumed, "Daddy sold our house today to some people named Gladstone. With Mommie gone, he doesn't want to live here anymore."

Julie cringed a little with an uncomfortable pang of conscience. How could she have been cruel to her one and only friend, who not only had lost her mother, but now had to move away?

In her mind's eye, Julie recalled the first time she had approached Genevieve, who was just three at the time. The little girl was playing in her sandbox, and Julie had come over the fence, fully intending to relieve the child of her bright blue shovel.

Genevieve looked up, smiled, and preempted her ploy with an invitation. "Wanna pway with my shovel?" she asked innocently, holding it toward Julie with her chubby little fingers.

"Uh... okay," Julie replied, dumbfounded by her neighbor's generous gesture. That afternoon was a first in Julie's life: she actually played peacefully with someone else. Of course, Genevieve did all the giving and Julie did all the taking, but Gen didn't seem to mind and Julie never even noticed. Thus began the strangest of friendships, a naughty neighbor and a nice one.

Genevieve was the exception to the rule in Julie's playbook. Other potential playmates were not as compliant, and soon shut her out of their games, so Julie contented herself with tormenting them from a distance, when she could find nothing better to do.

And now that Gen was leaving, she'd *really* have nothing better to do – no friend at all. "Well, I don't care," Julie decided, "I don't need anything or anybody."

That night, Julie cried herself to sleep, too proud to share her problem with her parents, and too hardened in her heart to realize that she *was* the problem.

Three weeks later, Genevieve and her father pulled away in their car for the final time. Gen was only moving to a nearby town, but neither child could read or write yet, so she might just as well have moved across country. Julie waved good-bye to Genevieve with her free hand; the other held Gen's favorite sea shell, a gift from the heart of her little companion.

Julie waited for the car to pull completely out of sight, then with bitter tears, pulled her arm way back, preparing to throw her treasure into the creek below. She thought better of her impulse, and gingerly placed the memento in the side pocket of her shorts.

Back in the house, Julie plopped down on the couch in the den, and stared mindlessly at the wall. Her mother, noticing her unusual behavior, asked, "Anything wrong, honey?"

"No," Julie lied, to her mother and to herself.

4

New Neighbors

One Saturday morning, a few weeks after Genevieve's departure, Julie was awakened by the rumble of another vehicle in the driveway next door. Her bedroom being located on that side of the house, Julie jumped up and carefully brushed the bedroom curtain aside, just enough to see a huge yellow moving van backed catercorner between the driveway and the double front doors of Gen's house.

Julie didn't twitch an eyelash as she watched the movers begin to unload the furniture from the van. Was that a white twin bed decorated with pink roses she saw being carried into the house? And a red tricycle, and a box of toys with a doll's arm hanging out?

She had seen enough. She already disliked whatever little girl had dared to take Genevieve away from her. She closed the curtain roughly and climbed into her jeans. "This should be fun," she mused to herself as she imagined her revenge on the new neighbor.

Meanwhile, David and Ruth Gladstone, with their four-year-old daughter, Rebecca, were pulling away from their duplex for the last time. Of course, Rebecca was too little to fully understand what was happening, but she knew from her mother that she would no longer be seeing Ricky and Judy, her two favorite playmates, on a daily basis. The fact that the families worshiped together on Sundays made the prospect of leaving them behind a little less painful, but Rebecca didn't know what to expect other than that.

"Mommie, if we don't like our new house," she asked, "can we go home?"

Her mother suppressed a laugh, knowing that the question was not funny to her little girl. "No, sweetheart," she began, "we have a new home now, with our own backyard, trees, a sandbox, and even a little swimming pool. Don't worry, Rebecca, God is looking after us and He will provide everything we need in our new surroundings."

Rebecca relaxed at her mother's reassurance, and contented herself with her favorite picture book in the back seat of the van, as the family made their way to their new home in Baysville.

"We're home, Rebecca," sang her mother from the front seat. Rebecca had fallen asleep with her book on her lap and opened her eyes drowsily to take it all in. The house was pretty, not very large, but certainly big enough for their small family. And the trees seemed to be begging for the addition of a backyard swing, just as her daddy had said.

The day was pleasantly cool for June, and after showing Rebecca where her room would be (after all the boxes were cleared away) her mother suggested that she and her doll, Molly, investigate the back yard. Having received careful instructions about staying within the fenced yard, Rebecca picked Molly up out of a nearby box, and skipped down the hall to the kitchen door.

Julie saw Rebecca before Rebecca saw her. Like a bobcat stalking its prey, Julie eyed the little girl who was meandering around the yard and then finally settling down to investigate the sandbox. Julie was indignant. *Who does she think she is, sitting in Genevieve's sandbox!*

A shadow suddenly appeared over the corner of the sandbox. Rebecca raised her head and was very surprised to discover that she was not alone. It seemed strange to her that another child would just appear suddenly. She had been taught to stay in her own yard unless invited to come to someone else's house.

Nevertheless, Rebecca smiled and greeted her visitor. "Hello, my name is Rebecca. What's yours?"

"It's Julie," the other child grudgingly replied. And then, swinging into her ugly plan, she added, "Can I see your doll?"

Rebecca hesitated for just a moment. To her, Molly was not a mere toy. Handing her doll to Julie was like giving someone she loved to a stranger. But Rebecca had been taught to share and meekly gave in to Julie's request.

"Sucker," Julie laughed, as she grabbed the doll and ran quickly away. Before Rebecca had a chance to react, Julie had already rounded the back corner of the house, thrown the doll into a window well on the side wall, and skipped merrily back home.

5

Let There Be Light

The Saturday Only Club jumped as one person
(including Grandma Greene and therefore a startled
Donnie) as the electricity suddenly flashed on
throughout the house. Grandma covered her mouth
with her free hand, so that the children could not see
her smothered laughter. Liza, the tweenage holdout,
had in the darkness inched her way from the far end of
the couch to a front row seat on the rug near the
storyteller. Not one of the children had noticed that
the wind was no longer howling.

"Well," suggested Grandma, "anyone for
foosball?"

"What'd Rebecca do about her doll?" asked
Emily, completely ignoring Grandma's teasing
question.

"Uh, I could use a break," offered an embarrassed
but honest Tommy. "But please don't tell anything till
I get back." The line was a long one down the hall as
the other children took advantage of Tommy's frank
admission.

Finally, they were all settled again. After taking a
sip of her stone-cold coffee, Grandma resumed her
story.

"Rebecca hopped up and ran after the thief, but
when she turned the corner, Julie was already opening
the front door to her own house. Tears flooding her

baby cheeks, Rebecca ran into her house to find her mommie."

Mrs. Gladstone was finally able to piece together the story between her daughter's sobs, and praying silently for wisdom, was able to comfort her child. "Rebecca, Jesus saw Julie take your doll. He knows you love Molly and He loves you. You just wait. God will take care of this situation and will take care of your dolly, too."

Then, taking her daughter's small hand in hers, Mrs. Gladstone prayed aloud, "Father, You see and know everything. Will You please bring Molly back to Rebecca? In Jesus' Name, amen."

"Amen," echoed Rebecca with faith and a few stray tiny tears.

Just then, there was a knock at the kitchen entrance to the house. Mrs. Gladstone jumped up to greet the immediate answer to her prayer. It was the neighborhood paper boy, with an account book in one hand, and Molly in the other.

"Hi," he said. "My name is Jeff. I saw that this house was occupied again, so I decided to stop by and see if you want a subscription to the newspaper. When I walked down the driveway, I spied a doll down in your basement window well, and figured you had a visit from Julie. Am I right?" He paused to hand Molly to Rebecca.

Seeing their nods, he continued, "Julie doesn't quite rhyme with bully, but that's just what she is. She did the same thing to my little sister last spring, only she threw her doll in the *bushes*. Good thing I came along, huh?"

"Thank you, Jeff. Actually you are the answer to a prayer," replied Mrs. Gladstone. Jeff wondered to himself how the credit suddenly shifted from him to prayer, but was delighted when Mrs. Gladstone signed up for the morning paper on the spot.

Rebecca hugged her *little girl* tightly, while Mrs. Gladstone hugged hers. It was quite a glad reunion. The conclusion to this incident did not come about quite so happily at Julie's house. Julie had skipped into her house chanting a ditty she had made up on the spot for the occasion.

Just in case her new neighbor was within hearing, Julie turned to face the open screen door, and sang, "Ha-ha-ha-ha-ha, where's your precious dolly now?" So enamored was she with the success of her mission, that she had not noticed her daddy's car in the driveway – nor did she see him critically observing her performance from the hallway.

"Whose dolly?" he bellowed. Mr. Greene had just come in from a three-week road trip, and was in no mood for Julie's mischief. Julie couldn't think up a good story to tell him, nor could she twist the truth quickly enough to her advantage.

That was the first and last time Julie ever went into the Gladstone's yard until the day six years later, when she fell into the creek and the Gladstones saved her life.

Meanwhile, she had to content herself with leaning over the fence and eying Rebecca jealously at

a distance. If she were absolutely sure her father was
not coming home, she might venture taunting Rebecca,
and later on, Sarah, with some unkind remark. But the
spanking her daddy gave her for taking her neighbor's
doll, made her wary of ever disobeying his rule:
"Don't you ever set foot in that yard again."

6

First Day – First Grade

The first day of school could not come soon enough for Julie. She was itching for mischief, and the dollar incentive her father offered the babysitter to report any future misbehavior when her parents were away from home was, from her perspective, crimping her style.

From God's perspective, Mr. Greene's attempt to discipline his daughter was the best thing that had ever happened to Julie. A little light entered her soul that day, and she learned there was a price to pay for going her own way. The incident was good preparation for Julie's entrance the following year into elementary school.

When enrollment day for first grade finally arrived, Julie was not quite as "itchy" to begin school as she had thought. Mrs. Greene had gotten permission from her boss to come in late to work on the opening day of school, so that she could accompany Julie to her classroom. Julie did not resist her mother holding her hand. Though she would never admit it, even to herself, entering a new school was just a bit frightening to the independent little girl.

Imagine Julie's surprise when she was greeted at the door by her new teacher, Mrs. Peach, with a warm welcome. "Well, Miss Pretty Brown Eyes, what's your name?" No one had ever told Julie she had pretty eyes, and she was completely caught off guard.

Unable to keep from smiling at her teacher, Julie answered rather meekly, "Julie Greene."

"Julie, I'm glad to meet you. You may take whatever seat you like." Only then did Julie let go of her mother's hand, and without giving it further thought, she ran for the table directly in front of the teacher's desk. Later, Julie would wonder why she did this, as it put her in a position of having her behavior easily observed.

Kindergarten had been a miserable experience for Julie. Her teachers there had tried to teach Julie the basic pre-reading skills, but Julie was trying just as hard to keep from learning anything. Sad to say, Julie won that battle.

Now, to her embarrassment, she was the only child in the first grade who could not at least recite the alphabet. That fact was discovered the very first day, when Mrs. Peach lined the children up to sing the alphabet song, having each of them take a turn singing a letter. The class giggled when Julie's turn came, because she did not know that the letter Q followed the letter P in the song.

Mrs. Peach quickly quelled the laughter. "Children, that's enough," she said in a gentle but firm voice. "Return to your tables," she added. And then as if to deliberately change the subject, Mrs. Peach took out her attendance book and announced to the class, "One of you has a birthday today."

Alexander blushed the same color as his bright red shirt, figuring correctly that the teacher was talking about him. Mrs. Peach continued, "Would anyone like to lead the birthday song?"

Julie gingerly raised her hand, hoping somehow to make up for her embarrassing moment.

"Thank you, Julie. Would you start the song now?"

"Happy birthday to you," began Julie, in a sweet melodic voice. Twenty pairs of ears heard the pleasant childlike sound, and then all the children joined together to sing to Alexander.

"Julie," remarked Mrs. Peach appreciatively after the song, "you have a lovely voice!" Twice in one day, her teacher had lifted Julie's spirits.

Maybe first grade won't be so bad after all, Julie mused to herself, and went home happy that day. She didn't even bother to position herself at Rebecca's fence for an afternoon catcall. She simply stayed in her room and relived the memory of Mrs. Peach's compliments.

That evening, Julie pulled out the little alphabet song record Mrs. Peach had handed her to take home. After listening to the song three times, Julie was able to sing the song without a single mistake. She was not only pleased with herself, but she was amazed that she could learn so quickly. So was Mrs. Peach.

The next morning, Julie ran into her classroom at the sound of the first bell, and with childish enthusiasm, greeted her teacher with her own musical rendition of the alphabet song. Later that day, Mrs.

Peach read Julie's personal file, and discovered that
Julie's potential for learning was way above average.
Good teacher that she was, she acted immediately on
this piece of information and handed Julie a special
book that very day.

Mrs Peach had made the little book herself. It
contained only three sentences, but it had 26 pages of
illustrations. Each page displayed an illustration of one
of the letters of the alphabet, and the three sentences in
the book had a total of 26 words; the first letter in each
word was in alphabetical order from A-Z.

As the children lined up for lunch that day, Mrs.
Peach whispered quietly to Julie, "Julie, could you
wait just a minute before going to the lunchroom?"
Julie nodded her head shyly, wondering what Mrs.
Peach would say to her. The rest of the children filed
out of the room with the lunch monitor, and Mrs.
Peach approached Julie with her handmade book. She
explained to Julie how the book was arranged, and
Julie quickly understood just how she was to read it.

"If you'll come back after lunch," continued Mrs.
Peach, "we can read the book together during recess.
Then you can take it home and practice on your own."
Julie agreed, and followed Mrs. Peach to the lunch
room. The little girl was so excited, she could hardly
swallow her grilled cheese sandwich and soup, even
though it was her favorite cafeteria meal.

In less than ten minutes, she was ready for her
appointment with the teacher, but Mrs. Peach had told
her to wait in the cafeteria until she came for her.

Finally, Mrs. Peach arrived and led Julie to the classroom.

The book was a little strange, but fun. Julie giggled as Mrs. Peach read her the three sentences illustrated on the 26 pages. The sentences were so unusual that Julie remembered them without even trying, and after only one time through, she was able to "read" the entire book. The picture of the fish driving down the road in a blue car made Julie laugh out loud.

Julie left school that day with a homework assignment. She was to read through the book ten times, paying close attention to the first letter of each word and repeating aloud, "B is for blue, C is for car," and so on. All the way home on the bus, Julie held the book tightly as she sang one of her little made-up ditties. She recited each sentence of her very own alphabet book in a sing-song fashion as the wheels of the bus kept rhythm down the highway.

"A Blue Car Drove Each Fish Going Home In June. Kids Like Marbles, Nuts, Oranges, Popcorn, Quarters, Rocks, Snacks, (and) Toys. Under Vick's Wagon Xavier Yelled Zoom!"

When the bus finally pulled up in front of Julie's house, she ran into her room, without even saying hello to the babysitter, and opened her precious treasure.

It was not a crazy daydream, she assured herself. The book was real. Mrs. Peach had given it just to her and she could read it. Of course, Mrs. Peach had explained that what Julie was doing was not really reading but was showing her what reading would be like if she ever learned how.

These thoughts occupied Julie's mind happily until supper. One thing she knew for sure, she *would* learn to read. And even more than the fun of reading was the fun of having Mrs. Peach's attention.

7
Giant Greene Clouds

For the first few months of school, Julie was having the time of her life. She learned to read more quickly than any of the other students, simply by giving her attention to Mrs. Peach's lessons on phonics. She patiently learned to sound out words syllable by syllable until she could read any sentence smoothly and with understanding. Then she was chosen by her teacher to coach some of the slower children; but as Julie's success grew, so did her head.

The students began calling her *teacher's pet* whenever Mrs. Peach was not around. Instead of being offended by that moniker, Julie was proud of it, and the other kids soon left her alone in her little world. But as long as Julie had her teacher's attention and approval, she didn't need anybody else, and continued her antics on the playground where Mrs. Peach could not see her misbehavior.

November brought a new student into Mrs. Peach's classroom. His name was Rodney, and when Julie noticed Mrs. Peach put her arm around his shoulder and introduce him to the children at his table, she immediately disliked him.

Mrs. Peach didn't seem to notice that Rodney had an unruly cowlick and was missing his front teeth. Julie really began to seethe when she saw Rodney going home the first day with the same special

handmade book Mrs. Peach had given her at the
beginning of the year. Giant Greene clouds of
jealousy were on the horizon, as Julie's naughty
imagination began to contrive a way she could get rid
of Rodney, or at least bring him down a peg or two in
Mrs. Peach's eyes.

The next day on the playground, Julie sidled up
to Rodney, and said sweetly, "Wanna play marbles?"

"Haven't got any," answered Rodney, his hands
digging down into his empty pockets.

"That's okay," Julie replied. "I have enough for
both of us." So the two children spent recess shooting
marbles in a little ring drawn in the dirt on the
playground. Julie couldn't wait to try her special trick
on Rodney, but she decided it would be better to string
him along for a few days.

By the end of the week, Rodney was following
Julie around the playground like a little puppy dog.
Being the new kid on the block, so to speak, he was
truly grateful for her attention. That day he discovered
Julie's terrible scheme.

"Hey Rodney," she began at recess, "do you ever
watch wrestling on television?"

"Sure," he said. "My dad watches the fights every
Saturday afternoon."

"Well," Julie continued, "let's play wrestling.
First, you take my arm and twist it around my back."

"I don't want to hurt you, Julie," said Rodney
hesitantly.

"You won't hurt me," Julie reassured him. "Just
pretend that you're holding my arm tightly."

"Okay," agreed Rodney. picking up Julie's arm and folding it gently behind her back.

Just then, a bloodcurdling scream was heard all over the play yard as Julie pretended that Rodney was really hurting her. The recess teacher rushed right over and noticed Rodney standing in a very incriminating position with his arm still holding Julie's against her back.

Rodney was too shocked to understand what was happening, until the teacher in charge grabbed him by the arm and marched him briskly into the school. Julie followed, loudly complainir.g, "He twisted my arm!" She even managed a few fake tears for the benefit of the teacher.

Rodney was still in a state of disbelief. Like a lamb led to the slaughter, he found himself seated outside of the principal's office, without a clue as to what he was doing there.

Fortunately for Rodney, Julie's reputation for bad behavior followed her from her kindergarten class. The case was dismissed for lack of believable evidence, and both children were given a stern warning that such games would not be allowed.

From that day on, Rodney eyed Julie nervously, and Mrs. Peach, though still kind and helpful, was somewhat distant toward her. Once again, Julie had destroyed her one hope of friendship.

Were it not for the books Julie checked out daily from the school library, she would have been one unbearably lonely little girl. But the more Julie read, the better she was able to read, and she was soon devouring books far beyond her grade level.

8

Finally, A Friend

By the time Julie was in the fourth grade, she had the reading level of a high school sophomore, and voraciously devoured every book she could get her hands on. She particularly liked Tom Sawyer and Huck Finn. Their escapades appealed to her independent nature and love of mischief. She vicariously enjoyed the fact that both characters seemed to get away with their misbehavior.

One day in the fifth grade, Julie was walking toward the exit door of the library, her arms filled with books she had just checked out. Coming in the door at the same time was another student, whose arms were equally overloaded with books he was bringing back. The two children collided, books scattered everywhere, and muffled laughter echoed among the usually quiet stacks of the library.

Julie was red-faced and furious. Naturally the fault lay with that idiot of a boy who had bumped into her. But once again, Julie was confronted with the fact that it takes two people to argue. When the boy without a word began to pick up all the books and hand them to her, Julie was dumbfounded. Then he opened the door so that she could leave. What was he up to? She'd have to think about that one for a while.

"You like to read?" The question came from the seat on the bus just behind Julie that same afternoon.

To her amazement, the boy she bumped into in the library evidently rode her bus. She'd never noticed him before. "My name is Ted Carroll," he offered. "I just moved here from Gainsborough. I'm the boy you bumped into in the library today."

"You mean you're the boy who bumped into *me*," Julie corrected with a slightly miffed expression on her face.

"Have it your way," he returned, not willing to let the conversation drop. "What kind of books do you read?"

The subject of reading was so enticing to Julie that she forgot her anger and answered him with interest. "Actually, most anything, but particularly Mark Twain books and biographies of famous people."

"Well, that's one thing we have in common; I like biographies too, especially about historical figures and inventors. Maybe you could suggest some books you've read that I might want to read, and I could do the same for you."

"Okay," Julie said. It struck her suddenly that Ted was new to the school and might not have heard of her past behavior. Julie really needed a friend. She was tired of the cold shoulder treatment from other kids, and sick of spending recess sitting on a bench reading alone. Anxious to seal the agreement with Ted, she sputtered out the first title that she could think of. "There's a book in the library on the life of George Washington Carver. I like that one a lot."

"Thanks," replied Ted. "See you in the library," he added, smiling, and sat back in his seat. Suddenly he sat up abruptly, and whispered, "You're okay – for a girl."

Most girls Julie's age would have been insulted by that remark, but Julie took it as a compliment. Boys her age seemed to think girls were usually empty-headed and prissy. She didn't mind it that Ted seemed to exempt her from that description.

Of course, this new friendship would cost her something. She would have to forgo making snide remarks on the playground, and other similar activities that a nice boy like Ted might disapprove of. It was time once again to keep the ugly side of her personality at home.

That idea would take some restraint on her part. Her next-door neighbors, the Gladstones, now ignored her presence at the fence completely. Ever since Sarah had made that unexpected reply to her "spilling the beans," taunting the girls was no fun anyway.

"Oh well," she sighed to herself, "I can always *read* on weekends."

9

A Baptism of Love

Julie had been badly burned when her plan to
unseat Rodney from Mrs. Peach's affections backfired.
She was not about to let the same thing happen again.
She had learned her P's and Q's in the first grade; she
was not about to forget the lesson.

Ted and Julie spent so much time together at
school that the other kids started to tease them. The
two buddies just ignored their teasing, preferring each
other's company no matter what anybody said.

They were even able to laugh themselves at the
dual moniker their classmates assigned to them. The
kids started calling them "four-eyes" – not because
they wore glasses, but because their four eyes were
always glued to books as they sat reading side-by-side
in the library, or under the trees on the playground, or
even occasionally in the lunch room. Julie was finally
enjoying a good relationship.

Then came that fateful winter day when Julie
nearly drowned in the icy creek. The incident changed
her life forever. She could no longer ignore the love
that caused the Gladstones to run to her rescue at the
risk of their own safety. She and her mother – and
then her father – did some serious thinking about their
lives after that near-tragedy.

Two weeks following the incident, Mrs. Greene
suggested to her husband, "Let's go to church,

Wayne," and Mr. Greene agreed without hesitation. He knew that something needed to change in their family.

Mr. Greene had tried to make a good living as a salesman, but he knew his family had suffered from the constant absences. He also sensed that they needed something else too – something their neighbors, the Gladstones, seemed to have.

The church near their neighborhood was friendly and inviting. The pastor was an older man. He was not an eloquent speaker, but he exuded a love for Jesus that could not go unnoticed. That morning he spoke on the subject of baptism. As the pastor described being "buried in baptism" and "rising again to walk in newness of life," Julie's thoughts immediately went to the icy creek.

Hey, she said to herself, *that's kind of like what happened to me, when I fell in the creek. When I came up out of the water and the Gladstones were there to save my life, I felt really different.*

Jesus touched Julie's heart that day in the service. As the pastor explained the plan of salvation, Julie remembered Rebecca's words from so long ago: "Julie, you need Jesus in your heart." Julie knew Rebecca was right. She was bad, and she *did* need Jesus in her heart.

As the congregation sang the invitation hymn, *Nothing But The Blood of Jesus,* Julie started moving toward the aisle. Her mom and dad got up as if to let her out, but then suddenly they were coming with her toward the front. They must have heard His call too.

That day, three new souls not only joined the family of God, but got a fresh start on being a family themselves. It made them all feel clean, like newborn babies.

The Greenes were eager to share the news with the Gladstones, but that would have to wait until their neighbors returned from a Christian conference. Meanwhile, the family just enjoyed each other. When they came home from the service that day, Mrs. Greene fixed a quick lunch and they all sat down together to eat. Mr. Greene gently reached for his wife's hand, and then Julie's, and they gave thanks as a family for the very first time.

Not only was the Holy Spirit on the move in the Greene household, but a giant whirlwind of change was coming to the Greene family. Mr. Greene immediately realized that he needed to be home every night. With that in mind, he decided to apply for a job in the home office. He knew it would take an act of Congress, or more likely a miracle of God, to get him such a position. Nonetheless, Mr. Greene went to see the company vice president early on Monday morning.

"We don't have anything available here in the office right now," Mr. Higgins told him, "but it's funny you should bring this up today. Just a few minutes ago I got a message that Mr. Wilson, the manager of our branch in Brighton, has contracted pneumonia. His doctor says it will be at least a month before he can work again, so I'll be needing someone to fill in for him until then. Now, Brighton is three hundred miles from here, and the assignment would be temporary.

But if you want it, it's yours. In the meantime, we'll be looking for a more permanent arrangement that might suit you better."

"Can I think about it?" asked Mr. Greene.

"Sure. Just let me know by tomorrow morning. I really hope we can work something out, Wayne. We hate to lose you as a salesman, but we certainly don't want to lose you altogether."

The three newborn Christians met together in a little huddle that evening. Julie felt very grown up being included in her parents' decision, as Mr. Greene explained the opportunity and dilemma facing them. "I don't want to turn down Mr. Higgins' offer, or he might think I'm not really serious about wanting a stationary post. But I can't see leaving you two again for even a month."

Having truly found each other at last, they all felt the same way about being separated again so soon. So, they decided to do something crazy. They would pack up whatever they could fit in the cars, drive to Brighton, and try to find an apartment to rent for a month. Julie could either keep up with her schoolwork in the apartment, or else try to fit in at the local elementary school for that short period.

"Mom, Dad," Julie announced with conviction, "I know Jesus must be in my heart. If He hadn't come in, I wouldn't be willing to leave. But my heart is so different. It makes me want to do whatever you say we need to do."

"Then I guess it's settled," said Mr. Greene. "I'll call the home office tomorrow and tell them I accept their offer."

Julie didn't sleep very well that night. She wasn't worried exactly, but perhaps a little nervous about the new adventure. The one thing that did bother her about leaving was telling Ted. She knew he depended on her friendship as much as she depended on his.

The next morning, before she left for school, Julie asked her mother if it would be okay for her to call Ted once a week from Brighton.

"Of course," her mother reassured her. "Julie, I'm really proud of the way you're taking this. You seem to be growing up overnight."

"You know, Mom, it's kind of fun to be different." Julie reached up and hugged her mother as naturally as if she had been doing it all her life. In reality, this was the first time she could remember.

When Julie got off the bus that morning, she ran immediately to the before-school meeting place she and Ted had agreed on long ago.

Julie told Ted the whole story, starting with the creek incident. After that, she told him that she and her family had visited a church on Sunday, and that they had all become Christians during the service.

Julie was surprised to see Ted's face light up with understanding. "Julie, I'm so glad for you," he interjected. "Now you're my real sister. I'm a Christian too."

That little piece of information made it easier for Julie to tell Ted the final part of her story. Gently, she began, "Ted, there's some bad news too. My family is leaving Baysville temporarily." Julie went on to explain about her dad's new job and why they had to leave.

Ted tried to take the news of Julie's departure like a man, but the little boy inside him wasn't holding up too well. He made some excuse for rushing off so that he could sort out his feelings by himself. Julie watched sympathetically as he turned away and went down the hall. Tears crept uninvited into her sad brown eyes as she remembered how awful she had felt when Genevieve moved away.

Julie then took all of her books out of her locker, as her parents had instructed, and reported to her classroom to get any assignments that might help her keep up.

When that was done, Julie called her mother to come pick her up. After they got home that morning, Mrs. Greene presented Julie with another task. Using the empty suitcases and boxes in her room, she was to pack up everything she could possible need for a month. As Julie was going through her possessions, she came across the little seashell Genevieve had given her. A thought came to her at once, which made her practically burst with joy even to consider. Hopefully, she approached her mother with a plan.

"Mom," she asked, "what time are we leaving tomorrow?"

"Well, Julie," answered her mother, "we want to get there as early as possible so we'll have time to get a place rented. So we need to be on the road by eight o'clock. Why do you ask?"

"Is there any way we could drop by the school tomorrow before the first bell? I need to see Ted one more time. It's really important to me, Mom. Please?"

"All right Julie. I'll ask your dad, but I'm sure he'll agree."

The next morning Mr. Greene climbed into his station wagon, which was stuffed with everything they could squeeze in, and pulled out of the driveway to begin the journey. Mrs. Greene and Julie followed close behind in the family car – which was also bursting at the seams. When they reached the school, Julie hopped out and ran straight to the meeting place. Ted was waiting there out of habit, but looked surprised to see her.

"I can't stay but a minute, Ted," she panted, and pulled Genevieve's seashell from her pocket. "Ted, this is my most precious possession. Just keep it till I get back. Oh, and I forgot to tell you – my parents said I could call you once a week. So I'll call you Thursday night at 7:30 every week if that's all right with you."

Ted was grinning from ear to ear, he was so glad to have a connection – any connection – to his friend. "Okay," he agreed eagerly. "By the way," he added, "you're still okay – for a girl."

Now Julie could leave with a song in her heart, and that's just what she did.

10

Walking By Faith

Just as new babies need everything done for
them, so the Greenes needed a lot of help starting their
new life as Christians. After locating an apartment, the
first thing they did was to find Antioch, a little church
in Brighton recommended by Pastor Goodman back in
Baysville. The pastor, Steven Seymour, happened to
be a personal friend of his from long ago.

Pastor Steve and the Antioch family welcomed
the Greenes with open arms. They not only stocked
their refrigerator with enough food for a week, but also
sent someone by to check on them each Monday
thereafter. Those times were precious, especially to
Mrs. Greene and to Julie, who knew no one in the
town and had no idea how to get around when Mr.
Greene was at work.

After a week or two, the Greenes began to get
used to their odd living arrangements. Julie looked
forward every Thursday night to calling Ted and
updating him on the situation. The first Thursday
night, she told him the story of the seashell. Ted was
pleased. Not only did Julie's gift show how much she
appreciated their friendship, but her story sounded like
something out of a novel.

"You know, Julie, you ought to write a book," he
remarked one Thursday evening.

"How does 'Marketta Twain' sound to you for a pen name?" she quipped, laughing. Julie silently marveled at her own ability to laugh – not *at* someone but *with* someone – and *at* herself. When she thought of all the ugliness of her past, it made her sad. But every time she thought on the miracle of Jesus living in her heart now, it made her happy all over again.

Julie was not the only one who noticed the radical change in her personality. In the early days of their friendship, Ted had gone past Julie's moodiness and sarcasm to make friends with her. He needed a friend, and they had something in common. Now he was reaping the benefits of his patience with all of Julie's faults. With her new life as a Christian, she was able to give, instead of just taking.

While Julie and Ted talked on the phone, Ted pulled the seashell out of his pocket and admired it once more. This seashell was a symbol of their friendship, and now that friendship would last for eternity.

Friday afternoon, Mr. Greene came home from work and practically leaped in the door. Mrs. Greene and Julie were in the kitchen preparing supper, and hearing his hearty greeting, the two emerged curiously from the kitchen. "Have a seat!" commanded the husband and father jovially. "That way you won't fall down, when you hear what I have to tell you."

They sat down obediently on the couch, and waited with bated breath. "*Well*," he began, "the former manager has recovered, but in the meantime the national office decided to give him a promotion.

And if you agree to *my* promotion, you are now looking at the new manager – that is, new *permanent* manager – of the Brighton sales office."

Two mouths flew open. Mrs. Greene was the first to speak, since Julie was stymied by conflicting thoughts. "Honey," she began, "as Pastor Steve would say, it seems like the Lord is on the move again."

"I thought you'd feel that way, Donna." Then Mr. Greene's eyes turned toward Julie, who was smiling and frowning at the same time, if that were possible. "What are you thinking about, Julie?" he asked her.

"Dad,'"she began, "I can't exactly explain how I feel. I'm so happy about our new life together that I don't want to put a damper on your excitement, but this is really going to be hard on both Ted and me. We are not only good friends, we're each other's only friend."

"I know it's hard for you, Julie," put in Mrs. Greene. "But just like we've been learning every day this last month, the Lord loves us and cares about every detail of our lives. He knows what you and Ted mean to each other as friends, and He knows just how to fill that void – for both of you."

"Thank you, Mom," said Julie. "Maybe this is part of what it means to 'walk by faith and not by sight,' like Pastor Steve told us last Sunday."

For the first time, Julie dreaded her Thursday night phone call with Ted. But before she could give him the news, Ted preempted her with a story of his own. "Julie, you're not going to believe this. Last

Friday it was rainy, and we had to stay in for recess. The teachers let us all go to the gym and kind of do our own thing. Naturally, I took the book I was reading, and found myself an empty corner. Do you remember Big Jake?"

"Sure," said Julie, "he's that boy with the stringy blond hair – the one who's already almost six feet tall."

"Yup, that's him all right. Well, he came over to where I was sitting, and playfully took the book from my hands. Then he said, 'Hey two-eyes, wanna shoot some baskets?'"

Ted couldn't help laughing over the phone as he recalled the moniker Jake had altered to apply just to him. "I found myself saying, 'Sure,' and got up – rather bravely, I might add – to face the basketball net for the first time in my whole life.

"Well, I picked up that basketball and threw it toward the basket as hard and high as I could. It must have gone a full three feet in the air."

Now it was Julie's turn to laugh. She could just picture her bookworm friend on the basketball court with Big Jake towering a foot over him, trying to shoot that basket.

"Jake laughed too," Ted admitted. "A little. But then he just said, 'Boy, do you need some lessons!' He grabbed the ball, and started to give me a few pointers just like he was a real basketball coach.

"Julie, it was really fun! I looked like an idiot, but I enjoyed trying. The best part of it is, I found out there's life after reading. Big Jake has been coming over to eat with me at lunch, and then we shoot baskets on the playground at recess. He's turning out to be a real friend."

"That's wonderful Ted," congratulated Julie. But inside her heart, Julie felt something she did not like. She didn't know what to call it, but somehow it made her feel like the old Julie. She decided to shelve it for the moment, as she still had to tell Ted her own news.

Ted took it in stride – *Perhaps too much in stride*, thought Julie to herself. Not willing to give Ted an inkling of the growing conflict within her, she promised to keep calling and perhaps to start writing. He assured her that he would write back, and would always look forward to her calls. Then they hung up.

That night, Julie slept poorly. She still couldn't pinpoint the problem, but she knew it bothered her that Ted had found a new friend. The next morning, as Julie was working on her school assignments at the kitchen table and her mother was preparing a salad for lunch, Julie suddenly burst into tears.

Mrs. Greene put the lettuce down and came over to her daughter, putting her arm gently around Julie's shoulder. "What's the matter, Julie?"

"Mom, Ted has a new friend in school, and when he told me about him, I felt bad instead of good, and it makes me feel awful to feel that way."

Her mother thought for a moment. "Julie, I think I know what the trouble is," she finally offered. "It's a problem you've had ever since you were a toddler. It's jealousy, Julie. Jealousy is something I know about from personal experience.

"When I was in high school, I dated a boy who was, from all appearances, what most girls would consider a "good catch." We started going steady, and I proudly wore his football sweater as well as his class ring.

"Shortly after he became my *steady*, I began to notice subtle changes in his behavior. After a while those changes became more obvious. He would blow up every time I said hello to a male classmate, and he even began making snide remarks about my spending so much time with my girlfriends.

"One day when I was going downtown with some other girls, I got the distinct feeling that I was being watched. The feeling was so strong that I turned around suddenly – just in time to see my boyfriend duck into a Woolworth's five-and-dime. Gradually he started following me everywhere I went, and after awhile he didn't even bother trying to hide it.

"Of course I didn't know the Lord then, and I didn't know how to extricate myself from the relationship. I just knew that Gary's jealousy and possessiveness were destroying both his life and mine.

"God must have been watching over me even then. After graduation, Gary was drafted into the Army. Because World War II was in full swing, he was sent overseas to Germany. While he was gone, I met your dad, who had just returned from the war, and we started dating.

"By the time Gary came back to the states with a German wife, your dad and I were married. The last I

heard about him, his third wife had left him too – and all because jealousy ruled his life.

"Jealousy is not only dangerous, Julie, it is sin. Remember what pastor Steve told us in a sermon about sin? All we have to do is agree with the truth, hate that sin like God hates it, confess it to Him, and He will take it out of our lives."

As Julie thought on her mother's words, several pictures came to her mind. One was of Scottie falling backward to the ground in preschool; another was of Rebecca and her doll; then of Rodney in the first grade; of Sarah, the basket baby; and finally of Big Jake. She hung her head in repentance. She no longer wanted anything to do with the old Julie and her jealousy.

Her mother's sound wisdom flooded Julie's spirit with peace. The truth had already set her free. Right then and there in front of her mother, she bowed her head again. "Father, I'm sorry for being jealous. Please cleanse me with the Blood of Jesus, and take this ugliness out of my life. In Jesus' Name I ask you, amen."

Julie then picked up her pen and continued her assignment. Her mother returned to the salad, cutting up carrots on the outside – rejoicing on the inside.

11

Tying Up Loose Ends

Mr. Greene came home from work that afternoon
with another inspiration. "The office is going to be
closed this Thursday and Friday for remodeling. How
would you girls like to go back to Baysville and get
the rest of our furniture and things from the house?"

"Yes!" they chorused in unison, but for entirely
different reasons. Mrs. Greene was thinking about
getting back all the things she had been doing without
for the past month. Julie's thoughts were of Ted first,
then of the Gladstones. They had talked on the phone,
but she hadn't seen them in person since the near-
drowning incident.

It felt strange for Julie to reenter her old house in
Baysville. It was something like "returning to the
scene of the crime," and it brought back memories that
were not so precious. But Julie knew what to do with
those memories now, and it made her glad all over
again that the old Julie no longer lived here – or
anywhere.

As soon as they arrived that evening, the Greene
family walked next door to see the Gladstones. They
were tired from their journey, but they were also
bursting with thanksgiving for this family who lived
out such a consistent Christian witness before them.

The Gladstones were not only at home, but
gathered in the living room for evening devotions.

Joyfully welcoming their neighbors into the house, they listened intently while the Greenes told what Jesus had done for them.

After they were finished, Julie turned to Rebecca and Sarah and said, "I'm so sorry for everything I ever said and did to hurt you. Will you forgive me?" In answer to her question, Rebecca reached out and hugged Julie. Then Sarah followed suit, and a wonderful time of fellowship began between the families. The Greenes and Gladstones parted that evening with a promise to keep in touch and to remember each other prayerfully.

The next day, Julie eagerly went to Baysville Elementary, first stopping by the office to turn in her books. She would be enrolling in a school in Brighton now, and no longer needed assignments from Baysville.

Then she ran to the playground to find Ted. And there he was, shooting some before-school baskets with Big Jake. Julie smiled happily when she saw them together. It made her feel good to know that she was now truly glad for Ted to have another friend.

Ted spied Julie at once. Dropping the basketball on Big Jake's toe, he shouted from the distance, "Hey Julie! I can't believe it's you!"

Julie quickly explained to both boys why she was there, that she couldn't stay long, but just wanted to say hello in person. Big Jake laughed, "Well, I haven't seen 'four eyes' in a long time. How ya doin'?" The three children talked together for a few more minutes, until the first bell rang.

Ted turned back and waved goodbye. "I've still got your seashell," he shouted.

"Don't lose it, two eyes," she returned, grinning. Thus ended that particular Baysville chapter in the life of the former backyard bully.

12

A Lick And A Promise

The Saturday Only Club jumped simultaneously
– again – as the timer on the stove rudely announced
the end of story time. Grandma Greene vaulted herself
from the rocker, handing a startled Donnie to Liza's
waiting arms. "Okay kids," Grandma said. "It's time
for a lick and a promise. You know what to do. To
your stations, everybody."

Donnie was wide awake now, and being unused
to the routine, asked innocently, "Grandma, what's a
lick and a promise?"

Grandma answered quickly, "In five minutes,
your parents will start arriving to pick you up. Now
each of us has a little job to do to get the house
presentable. Whenever you straighten something up in
a short time, you call it giving the job 'a lick and a
promise'. Since you are new to our little club, Donnie,
all you have to do is be sure that you are ready
yourself and then just watch everybody else. Next
week I'll think of the job for you to do." Grandma
then began the countdown: "100-99-98-97...."

Donnie watched wide-eyed while each child
hurried about the house. Liza filled the dishwasher
with the things from the cookie and milk snack;
Phoebe and Peter grabbed a waste paper basket at the
exact same time and proceeded to try to carry it in

opposite directions; Emily wiped off the kitchen cabinets; Tommy straightened up the living room.

"11-10-9-8-7-6-5-4-3-2-1.... " Grandma finished the count just as the children plopped down on the furniture, breathless and laughing. They obviously loved this little routine, not only because it was a challenge to finish in time, but because they were able to help Grandma in a practical way.

"So is that the end of the story, Grandma?" asked Emily hesitantly.

"Oh no," answered Grandma emphatically. "That's only the beginning,"

"Phew, that's a relief!" added Tommy, and then blushed at his own enthusiasm.

One by one the parents arrived to pick up their children – all except Emily's mother. She called to say that she would be late, as she had to go by the hospital to check on Emily's father, who was recovering from surgery. "I hate to impose on you, Grandma," said Mrs. Nichols, "but could Emily eat supper at your house tonight?"

"Why yes, of course," agreed Grandma readily. "Emily and I will have a great time. Don't worry about a thing."

Emily was glad for more than one reason that she would be having supper with Grandma. The leftovers they had were always great, but more importantly, there was something Emily needed to talk about – something that had been burdening her all day.

Within half an hour, the kitchen smelled like heaven and Emily's mouth was watering. Fried

chicken, fried squash, green beans, and sliced garden
tomatoes soon graced Grandma's kitchen table.
Grandma was not the world's best housekeeper, but
she was the world's best cook – or at least Emily
thought so.

After buttered biscuits and molasses for dessert,
the two companions retired to the living room, stoked
the fire, and sat down to chat. It always amazed Emily
that Grandma seemed to know when someone needed
to talk.

"Well, we're through eating, Emily. Now what's
eating *you*?" quipped Grandma.

Emily smiled at Grandma's corny little play on
words, but then her brow furrowed. "Grandma, the
story you were telling today about Julie really hit
home with me. My problem is not the same as hers,
but since I got saved last month, something's really
been bothering me."

"What is it, Emily?" asked Grandma gently.
"You know I'm always ready to listen."

"Well, last week I was cleaning out my closet,
and back in the bottom corner was my little treasure
box. I've had that box since I was five years old. I sat
down on my bed and took each item out. Grandma,
there were ten items in that box, but one of them was
stolen."

Grandma did not change her expression, but
continued listening intently as Emily poured out her
heart. "Grandma," Emily confessed, "that stolen item
belongs to you. In your jewelry box, you had a small
green ring. It was such a little thing, I told myself it

didn't matter – you wouldn't care. But now in my heart, I know the truth. I stole that ring from you. Grandma, can you ever forgive me?"

Grandma slipped her arm around a broken-hearted Emily. "I forgive you, Emily, with all my heart. What you have done just now in telling me the truth is a cause for rejoicing. The Lord Jesus rejoices, your parents will rejoice, I rejoice, and most of all, when you see this confession from God's perspective, you will be rejoicing yourself.

"In the book of Proverbs it says, 'He that covereth his sins shall not prosper, but whoso confesseth and forsaketh them shall have mercy.' It also says in First John that 'if we confess our sins, He is faithful and just to forgive us our sins and to cleanse us from all unrighteousness.' Both of those promises are given by your Heavenly Father, and they apply to you because you are his child. That's it, Emily. You're free!"

It was then that Emily's tears really began to flood. She reached her arms around Grandma's neck and cried until there were no tears left. Grandma rocked her gently until it was all out.

"It's funny," Emily said. "All afternoon I kept shutting out the truth, and I was more and more miserable. Now I feel happy – even lighthearted."

The two "*sisters,*" one old and one young, knelt together on the worn rug, and thanked their Father in heaven for sending Jesus to take our sins to the cross and leave them there.

Just then the doorbell rang, and Emily's mother had arrived. On the way home, Emily shared with her mother all that had happened. Meanwhile, Grandma did her dishes, but with her mind elsewhere. Her story was already bearing fruit. Another sinner had found victory.

13

New Beginnings

The Saturday Only Club could hardly wait to reconvene the following week. Tommy arrived at 9 a.m. on the dot. He had brought a sleepover friend with him, Charlie Evans. "Grandma," he blurted out rapidly as she opened the door, "Charlie spent the night at my house last night and I told him the whole story. He was supposed to go home this morning, but he asked his mother if he could come with me instead. He wanted to find out for himself what happened next. Is that all right?" Only then did Tommy dare pause to breathe.

Grandma laughed out loud at Tommy's unnecessarily dramatic plea. He knew good and well that it would be more than all right. Some people, as the saying goes, never meet a stranger. Grandma never met a child she didn't automatically love. "Come on in," she grinned at the boys. "The best seats in the house are waiting for you two early birds."

Then, as if the matinee movie were starting, Grandma's house began to fill up with the rest of the club all at once. A cup of cocoa apiece later, the occupants of the living room suddenly assumed an expectant hush. "Hope they're not going to be disappointed," Grandma chuckled to herself. Then, taking her place in the old rocking chair, she resumed the story.

"Last week," she reviewed, "Julie and her family had left Baysville for good, and were now beginning their new life in Brighton."

Mr. and Mrs. Greene decided that it was time to enroll Julie in the local elementary school. Since Mr. Greene had to be at work during school hours, the task fell to Julie's mother. She had not worked outside the home since the day they left Baysville. It was a financial stretch to be sure, but she and her husband felt strongly that she should be home for Julie every day.

After looking at Julie's excellent academic reports, the elementary school principal offered a simple suggestion. "Mrs. Greene, if I were you, I would just keep Julie out of school for the rest of the year. With so little time left, it just doesn't make sense to enroll her now – especially since she will begin junior high in the fall."

The concept of junior high was new to Julie, as the much smaller town of Baysville did not have it. Students went to elementary school, grades one through seven, and then entered high school in the eighth grade. At least now Julie would have the whole summer to get used to the idea of entering that world two grades early.

That summer turned out to be truly healthy in every respect, for both Julie and her parents. Antioch Church had only fifty members in its congregation, but three of that number were around Julie's age, and loneliness became a thing of the past for this formerly cheerless child.

One of Julie's favorite experiences over the summer was Vacation Bible School. She and her new friend Jennie particularly liked Morning Sing. The children all had breakfast together in the little church kitchen, then went into the sanctuary. For the next half-hour, the rafters rang with childlike enthusiasm, as the younger set bounced from chorus to chorus, praising the Name of Jesus in one continuous medley of song.

All of this was new to Julie. But she was a natural as far as music was concerned, and readily picked up both the melody and the lyrics of each song, chosen spontaneously by the different children present. Julie's favorite chorus was *Give me oil in my lamp, keep me burning.* The change in Julie's life since she had become a Christian was so radical, it was not hard for her to remember how much she needed that "oil" on a daily basis.

Another part of VBS that Julie particularly enjoyed was the Bible competition called "Sword Drill." The lineup of kids waiting to begin was a bit comical, since all ages competed at the same time. Seven-year-old Jonathan, barely four feet tall and wearing giant horn-rimmed glasses, stood next to the beanpole Andrew, who was 5'10" and, at fourteen, the oldest contestant.

Each child had the same kind of Bible, distributed from the Sunday school supply. Every contestant stood as still and silent as a soldier, waiting for the first of three instructions.

"Attention." At this first command, all the kids stood even taller and straighter, with their Bibles at their sides, not blinking an eyelid, lest they be disqualified.

"Draw swords," came the second instruction. Each contestant brought his Bible waist high and placed one hand on top and the other hand on the bottom of the closed volume.

At this point in the competition, the verse to be looked up was announced: "The first verse is Isaiah 9:6."

Finally the third instruction was given, "Charge." Suddenly there was a sound like a flock of geese flapping their wings, as the children flipped through the thin pages of the Old Testament to find the passage. First to find the verse was Carrie, who stepped forward and patiently waited for the moderator to call on her to read the passage.

And so the competition continued, as each child's score was recorded on the Sunday school blackboard behind the line-up. Twenty-five verses later, Carrie, Andrew, and little Jonathan each had five points. The other children were asked to sit down while they had the runoff. Julie watched from the sidelines nervously, just as if she were in the final competition herself. The moderator had decided that this verse would be the tiebreaker.

"Attention. Draw swords. Habakkuk 2:14," he announced with all the flair of a dramatic drum-roll. Then he seemed to pause for effect before giving the final instruction: "Charge."

Jonathan, the shortest, the youngest, and the least expected to succeed, stepped forward after only twenty seconds. Julie's eyes immediately went to Andrew to see how he was taking it. Andrew's smile was genuine. She could tell that he was sincerely glad for Jonathan.

Julie learned more than one lesson in that initial Bible drill. She learned that there was a lot of fun to be had in the simple things, but more importantly, that you can win, even when you lose.

The summer passed too quickly for Julie. Not only had she had a wonderful time and made several new friends, but she was discovering that the Bible was her favorite book. Every word was new to her, each story had an ending to be discovered.

She found herself waking up every morning with a sense of anticipation to face the day. The old Julie would have had to be dragged out of bed at the last possible minute, but the new Julie found her hand gravitating to the beautiful Bible beside her bed.

After her baptismal service in Antioch Church, Pastor Steve had handed her a burgundy leather bound Bible as a gift from the church. He had suggested that she read at least a verse every morning, beginning with the Gospel of John. This particular day, Julie read a whole chapter. She found herself needing more comfort than usual.

This would be her first day at Buford Junior High School, and she didn't know what to expect. It helped that Jennie attended the same school. They both would be lowly sixth-graders, and that fact in itself was intimidating. The two girls prayed, literally, that God would give them at least one class together.

The first bell sounded and the girls reported to the auditorium, where they were handed their schedules. Julie and Jennie clapped their hands together when they realized that they were in the same homeroom. Other than homeroom, they only shared physical education. But that was better than nothing, and at least they had the same lunch schedule. All sixth-graders ate at the same time.

The first three months at Buford Junior High passed without any major unpleasantness. Her classmates were not like her friends at Antioch Church, but at least her reputation from elementary school had not followed her to Brighton. A clean slate was certainly something to be grateful for.

Julie managed to get along well with all her classmates except one. "Mad Michael Murdock" was not tall, but he was stocky, and muscular for a twelve-year-old. He did not wear a tee-shirt saying, "Don't mess with me, dude" – but he might as well have.

No one understood this loner like Julie herself, but nothing she said or did seemed to shrink the chip on his shoulder. If she said "Excuse me" when she had to get by him in the classroom, he would disdainfully mock her with his own *excuse me*." If she tried to smile at him, he would snarl "What are you grinning at?" Had Julie herself not been such an impossible case the first twelve years of her life, she would have given up.

Sunday morning at 9:25 was prayer partner time at Antioch church. Each twosome or threesome found an empty pew or corner, and shared their burdens with each other and the Lord. Jennie was Julie's partner, and being familiar with Mad Michael herself, fully understood what Julie was up against.

Pastor Steve had taught them to talk to the Lord like a father – to tell Him what was wrong, and ask Him to fix it. So in the Name of Jesus, they left their burden before the throne.

Monday morning was blustery and cold for mid-November. The students were allowed to gather in the cafeteria before school, provided they remained seated at tables. Jennie and Julie were quietly talking together in the corner, when suddenly they heard the sound of spattering glass from the entryway.

Buford Junior High was a very old building, and the cafeteria had swinging doors with glass panes in the top half. Michael Murdock never opened any door – he always barreled through it like a football tackle. But on this particular day, his hand slipped off the wood and punched through the glass.

There stood Michael, his wrist bleeding profusely, and not a teacher in sight. Some of the kids, mostly boys, were laughing. Others just sat there staring.

Without thinking, Julie ran over to Michael, gave him her hankie, and told him to press it hard against his wrist. Then she suggested to the panicked boy that they should get to the first aid station down the hall as quickly as possible.

Too dazed to resist Julie's attentions, Michael followed as she opened the door. When they arrived at the station, the school nurse thanked Julie for acting so quickly. Then, after getting his wrist bandaged, Michael was sent to the hospital for stitches.

Julie assumed that to be the end of the episode, and rather dreaded running into Michael again, lest he make something ugly out of her attempt to help.

The next day, Michael sheepishly entered homeroom, his hospital bandage clear evidence that he had been seriously hurt. He didn't say a word of thanks to Julie, but as they were leaving the classroom, he stepped back for her to go ahead of him. *Small victories are sometimes the sweetest*, thought Julie, as she headed to physical education class to share the answered prayer with Jennie.

14

The Thanksgiving Choice

The week following the incident with Michael Murdock, Julie's English teacher gave the class some unusual homework. "Tonight, you have a writing assignment," announced Mrs. Bowen.

Twenty-five *ughs* echoed throughout the classroom. The only student not upset was Julie. She loved to write. To her it would be a pleasure, no matter what the subject.

The class was relieved to learn that there was no minimum word count. They had only to sit in a quiet room, with a pen and piece of paper, and write down everything they could think of to be thankful for. They were on their honor to sit there for a full half-hour and think, if nothing else.

The next day, Mrs. Bowen told the class that they would read their assignments aloud. Starting at the end of the alphabet, she called first on Audrey Zurich, who cringed. "May as well get it over with," she groaned as she came forward with her paper. "I am thankful that we finally had a short homework assignment," she read. "The end."

The class laughed out loud, while Mrs. Bowen stifled her own amusement. Next was George Young. He shuffled through his notebook, finally producing a wrinkled piece of paper that looked like it had been in a tug-of-war with a pit bull. "I'm thankful for the pinball machine I'm getting for Christmas," he mumbled. "I'm also thankful that my parents didn't catch me when I found it in the closet."

Again, the class roared with laughter. This assignment was not turning out the way Mrs. Bowen had expected. Instead of continuing through the alphabet to call on students, she asked for volunteers who had a paragraph or more to share.

Betty (referred to as "butter-up butter-cup" behind her back) raised an eager hand and came to the front. "I am grateful for having a terrific English teacher, who makes the class soooo interesting, and makes everything soooo easy to understand. I am also thankful that I didn't get Mr. Long for English because...."

Mrs. Bowen interrupted Betty at this point with a sigh of frustration. "Please pass your papers to the front, and use the rest of the class period for reading. I will read over the papers, and if I find one worthy of sharing aloud, I'll let you know."

The children were sobered at this, but relieved that they didn't have to read their papers out loud. The class was quiet until two minutes before the bell, when Mrs. Bowen suddenly lifted her head. "Now class, I have a paper to read from someone who did the assignment just as I asked. I will read it to you."

"I am thankful for my home, my parents, my friends, and my church. I'm grateful to be able to see, to hear, to walk, to sing, and to laugh. I also appreciate being able to live in a country where we have freedom to speak, freedom to worship, and freedom to make our own choices. For these gifts I am thankful to God, our Creator and the Giver of all good things."

The classroom suddenly became as still as a chapel. Though Mrs. Bowen did not announce who the author was, the blush in Julie's face did. Mercifully the bell rang just then and broke the awful silence.

During lunch break, Julie tried to gauge her classmates' reactions. Three girls whom Julie knew fairly well were giggling in the hall when she walked by. Was it her imagination, or did she hear one of them say, "I didn't know she was *religious*."

Just then, Jennie caught up to Julie in the hallway, and they went together into the cafeteria. While Julie was quietly telling Jennie what had happened, they were interrupted by Cecelia, the girl who sat behind Julie in English class.

"Wow!" she whispered as she leaned over them. "You made the rest of us look really bad with that great paragraph. But I wouldn't use words like 'worship' and 'God' around here if I were you. You're just asking for it."

As the afternoon went on, it became obvious that Cecelia was right. All of Julie's classmates looked at her differently, and probably would from now on. Julie knew that she had made her choice. Jesus had cleansed her from her sins and given her a way out of her ugly self. She could never keep quiet about Him, no matter what. She would just have to deal with the consequences one day at a time.

15

Old Friends

After the Thanksgiving incident, Julie was even more grateful for Jennie, a best friend who shared her beliefs and would always be there for her. Besides, Jennie possessed a rare quality: she knew how to listen. Most friends would hear what you said with their ears, but only long enough to chime in at the first pause with their own story. Jennie listened with her heart as well as her ears, as if what was being said *was* her story. God was so good to have brought Jennie into her life.

But Julie still had room in her life for one other best friend, the one in Baysville – Ted. They had agreed that it was not practical to keep calling each other every week by phone, now that she was going to stay permanently in Brighton. Long distance was too expensive for their allowances. So they decided to write once a week and take turns calling on holidays. Thanksgiving was just around the corner, and Julie could not wait to hear from Ted.

The phone rang early Thanksgiving morning. Julie just knew it was Ted, and picked up the phone immediately.

"Happy Thanksgiving!" The voice was deeper, but still Ted. Julie smiled, knowing from personal observation that the boys in her class were experiencing a change in their voices as well.

Julie had many things to share with her old friend, but she waited for him to give her a complete update on himself before launching into her own long story.

"Julie, you're not going to believe this," Ted told her, "but I have skipped a grade. My reading scores were so high on the performance test that the teachers thought I should go on to seventh grade. So here I am, the youngest kid in the class.

"The nicest part about the whole thing is that Big Jake is in the seventh grade too, since he's a year older than I am. So now we can have some classes together, as well as lunch and recess."

"Ted, I am so happy for you. You know the Bible says that 'all things work together for good to those who love God,' and this just shows it. Both of us have benefited from being separated. You've got Big Jake, I've got Jennie, and we still have each other."

It was a good thing that long-distance rates were cheaper on the holiday, because a full half-hour passed before either of the friends could bear to say goodbye.

Before they finally hung up, Julie shared with Ted about the Thanksgiving paper and the stir it had caused at school. Ted had not had any such experience himself, but he knew that very few of his fellow students felt about God the way he did. But there was one bright spot, he confided to Julie: Big Jake had begun going to church with him, and God seemed to be moving in his life.

"Jennie and I are prayer partners," Julie told him, "and we will be praying for you, and for Big Jake."

With that final note of encouragement, the old friends said farewell and promised once again to write. God's plan for each of them would be a page He would have to write Himself.

16

One Family Under God

Thanksgiving dinner at the home of the Greene family was the first any of them could remember where they were all together. In times past, Mrs. Greene would usually work on Thanksgiving Day to take advantage of the overtime, and Mr. Greene was often away on one of his extended sales trips.

Mrs. Greene decorated the table as if company were coming. Lately she was showing a side of her personality that Julie had never seen before: she was a natural-born homemaker. This aspect of her character, long suppressed by her busy-ness in the working world, now showed itself in surprisingly imaginative ways daily.

For the last hour before Thanksgiving dinner, Julie and her father were confined to the family room. When Mrs. Greene finally let them into the dining room, Julie felt like crying – it was all so beautiful. All three places at the table were adorned with Mrs. Greene's finest wedding china, crystal goblets, and sterling silver dinnerware. Candlelight in the center of the table enhanced the elegance of the scene.

Mrs. Greene was standing behind her chair. Julie followed her dad to the table and stood respectfully behind her chair, as did her father.

"Wayne," began Mrs. Greene, "when I was a little girl, my granddaddy always came to

Thanksgiving dinner at our house. He insisted that we all stand behind our chairs and, one by one, name something we were thankful for that day. Then he would pray the sweetest blessing over our food. That was the only time of the year I can ever remember my family praying or giving thanks. Would it be okay if we did that now?"

"I think that's a wonderful idea, Donna," her husband agreed. "I'll go first. I'm thankful for this lovely table, and for being home to enjoy it."

"I'm thankful," offered Julie through tears, "that the *old* Julie did not move to Brighton."

Finally, Mrs. Greene spoke. "I am grateful that the Lord has given us a new life, and has made our family one in Him."

The three joined hands as Mr. Greene offered a Thanksgiving blessing on the food. When they sat down, Julie noticed a small wicker cornucopia next to her plate. In it were miniature likenesses of fruits and vegetables, lovingly crocheted by her mother. Her daddy was busily admiring the one next to his plate. Julie would remember that lovely Thanksgiving dinner all her life, down to the minutest detail.

After the family had washed the last dish, they went back into the living room. In Mr. Greene's recliner was a brightly decorated orange and yellow package. On the loveseat, Julie spied a festive rectangular package as well, with her name on it.

The rest of the evening, the family played with the new deluxe Scrabble game Julie had received, and Mr. Greene rested his tired feet in the luxurious fur-lined house shoes his wife had scoured the city to find. What a day they had! What a wonderful Lord!

17

Growing Pains

Not every day was a "happy" one for the Greenes as new Christians. Babies have to learn to walk, and sometimes they fall and hurt themselves.

When Julie and Jennie returned to classes after the holiday, they were relieved that the Thanksgiving paper incident seemed to have been forgotten. Penelope Stone, the most popular girl in the sixth grade, had even invited both girls to her New Year's Eve party. Julie was jubilant. This would be her first party, and it felt good to be included.

She never dreamed that the invitation could bring her such grief. The day Penelope had invited them, Julie couldn't wait to get home and tell her mother.

She was a bit surprised when her mother didn't seem to share her enthusiasm. Gently, but rather soberly, she told Julie, "We'll have to see what your father says tonight."

Julie's balloon was not exactly popped, but it certainly had a slow leak as she waited for her father to come home. Mr. Greene's reaction to the party was somewhat stronger than her mother's. "Absolutely not," he answered without hesitating.

Julie was shocked. She hadn't even given any thought to *asking* her parents permission. She just assumed that because she wanted to do it, it was all right. Now she found the word *NO* imprinted boldly on her plans, and rebellion was at the door of her heart.

Without waiting to find out why her parents felt this way, Julie turned on her heel and ran to her room. She did not even come out for supper, but stayed in her room all evening, fuming and feeling sorry for herself.

It was the worst night of Julie's life since she became a Christian. She felt like two different people were fighting inside her, and the battle made her almost physically sick. She paced the room, then finally threw herself face-down on her bed, intending to burst into dramatic tears. But her own clumsiness ruined the melodrama, as the impact shook her bedside table and caused her Bible to fall noisily in the floor.

Julie saw the Book lying askew and reached down to pick it up. As she did so, she noticed the Scripture reference inscribed on the flyleaf – Ephesians 6:1. Julie had turned past that inscription many times before, but never looked up the verse. Curiously she looked it up now, and the words seemed to jump from the page. "Children, obey your parents in the Lord: for this is right." So simple, yet so convicting. Julie knew Who had to win this battle.

It was now midnight. Julie hated to wake her parents, but her heart was bursting with conviction. It simply could not wait until morning.

Running like the prodigal into their bedroom, Julie found her mother and daddy already awake. They had been praying for Julie, not knowing what else to do. Tearfully she spilled out her remorse, confessing her rebellion and asking their forgiveness.

Another reunion took place that night, as fellowship was once again restored – and sweetened by the truth.

The next day Julie shared with Jennie what had transpired. Jennie was not at all surprised at the Greenes' decision. Her own parents would have said the same thing, if she had bothered to ask. But Jennie had been a Christian longer than Julie, and she knew in her spirit that the party was not the right choice.

Julie was glad that she could be completely honest with Jennie, without the risk of losing her friendship over anything they might share. There was also a certain camaraderie in knowing that Jennie, too, would be staying home from the party.

Then Jennie popped a surprise of her own. "Julie, I asked my mom if you could spend New Year's Eve night at our house. She thought it was a great idea."

Julie's face lit up with joy – but she was mindful to remember the lesson she had so painfully learned. "I have to ask my mom and dad first," she answered thoughtfully.

"Of course," agreed Jennie, assuming that was naturally the next step in any plan.

Julie's heart was free and happy. She had made the right choice with her parents, and they were more than glad for her to spend the night with Jennie on New Year's Eve.

The girls had a wonderful time at Jennie's house, doing all the things that twelve-year-old girls find interesting. Jennie's parents had unexpectedly given the girls permission to stay up and greet the new year. But they laughed heartily at themselves the next morning, realizing that they had talked themselves to sleep five minutes before midnight.

If any questions remained about Penelope's party, they were clearly answered when school resumed in January. Rumors were flying that one of the boys had gotten into the Stones' liquor cabinet, and imbibed so much gin that he had to be rushed to the hospital.

Later, the girls learned that Penelope had planned special "refreshments" for them, if they had come. Cecelia had heard Penelope plotting with friends: "Wonder how those two Sunday school girls would act with a little vodka in their cokes!" Julie now had one more thing to be thankful for, and the new year was just beginning.

18

Springing The Mousetrap

After the New Year's incident, Julie and Jennie
began to exercise even more discretion in choosing
their friends. As they matured, both in years and in the
Lord, they began to see relationships more from his
perspective, and less through the lens of their own
inclinations.

Cecelia, the former informant, proved to be a
good and trustworthy friend, and regularly joined them
for lunch. Later, the three became four with a very
unlikely addition.

Melinda, "The Mouse," as they affectionately
called her, today would be termed a social misfit. She
was shyness personified, and no one could get a word
out of her. At roll call, the teachers had to look to see
if she were present, because raising her hand was
about as much communication as Melinda could
manage.

Julie, Jennie, and even Cecelia, decided to take
Melinda on as a project. Without requiring verbal
assent from the Mouse, the girls invited her to join
them for lunch one day. They were surprised when
she actually showed up!

But the real victory came at the close of eighth
grade, when they talked Melinda into walking up on
stage to receive her junior high diploma. That

promotion day came and left before any of them could believe it had finally arrived.

High school years were much more of a challenge than junior high, as childhood slowly slipped away. Teenagers of their generation, particularly the eighteen-year-old boys, were forced to face circumstances beyond their level of maturity.

The year Julie became a sophomore, the Vietnam War was raging in Southeast Asia. The draft was in full effect, and senior class boys were doing their best to get into some kind of college in order to avoid it.

The sixties brought other upheavals as well. The President of the United States was assassinated, teenagers were beginning to experiment with all kinds of drugs, and rock 'n roll idolatry had overtaken the country.

Antioch Church had not grown significantly in membership since the Greene family joined, but the bonds of Christian love there had become stronger and deeper with each passing year. In addition to the small prayer groups on Sunday morning, people would bring their burdens before the entire fellowship, and would see the Lord move mightily to answer.

Among their personal answers to prayer, Julie and Jennie rejoiced to see that Cecelia and her whole family had begun attending Antioch Church. And then one Sunday they spied Melinda being dropped off at the front door. The girls rushed over to make her feel welcome, wondering who was the stranger in the car.

The next day at lunch, Melinda suddenly spoke up as if she had been talking for years. "My foster

mother says that she'll bring me to church again this
Sunday if someone else can give me a ride home."

Those words were a heavenly symphony of
twenty-two notes to the other girls. Nothing else was
said that day by Melinda. After three separate offers
from her friends to see about getting her a ride home,
the conversation concluded in silent rejoicing.

Julie approached her mother that night to ask if
they might take Melinda home after the Sunday
service. Mrs. Greene agreed readily, knowing that her
husband would also. She knew as little about Melinda
as the girls themselves did – only that she never talked
– but she could see that Julie loved her silent friend,
and that was enough.

On the way home from church that Sunday, Mrs.
Greene surprised Julie by inviting Melinda to Sunday
lunch the very next week. They were all delighted
when the Mouse once again ventured a barely-audible
response: "I'd like that."

The Sunday invitation became a standing one
every week. Mrs. Carver, Melinda's foster mother,
was more than happy to find some companionship for
her. Her own best efforts to communicate with
Melinda had failed completely.

One weekend a few months later, Julie once again
approached her parents with a suggestion. "Mom and
Dad, what do you think about inviting Melinda to
spend the weekend with us?"

"Absolutely!" remarked her dad with unusual
enthusiasm. Remembering the time four years earlier
when he had answered the exact opposite with such

resolution, Julie smiled to herself – she must be on the right track this time.

Melinda was thrilled with the idea. (Julie could tell by the slight upturn at each corner of Melinda's lips.) Plans were made for Mr. Greene to pick up Melinda on his way home from work Friday evening. Melinda didn't even flinch at *that* suggestion, so she must really want to come.

The visit was an immediate success. The family loved having Melinda in their home, and she obviously loved being there. On Friday night, they all gathered around the television to watch an old movie called *The Sun Comes Up*. The story was about a fourteen-year-old orphan boy and his desire to have a mother. Afterward Melinda seemed pensive, even for her.

As soon as the movie was over, the girls got ready for bed. By interesting "coincidence," the previous owner of the house had left twin beds in the room that became Julie's.

It was late, and Julie drifted off quickly. Being a heavy sleeper, she did not hear the soft weeping in the other corner of the room. Julie's mother, however, was such a light sleeper that she could be awakened by the slightest noise. It was she who heard the muted tones of Melinda's distress. Softly she entered the girls' room and very gently touched Melinda on the shoulder. "Why don't you put on your robe," she whispered, "and come out to the family room."

Melinda nodded gratefully and soon joined Mrs. Greene on the loveseat. Then the floodgates opened. Mrs. Greene did not have to coax Melinda to tell her what was wrong. Melinda's heart was so full, she could no longer contain herself.

"When I was ten years old," she whispered, "my dad left my mother for another woman. My mother was so depressed, her doctor put her on medicine. But it just made her go downhill.

"Mom became so dependent on pills that she went to a lot of different doctors every week, trying to get more.

"One night she didn't come home. I was so worried and scared, I finally called the police. They found her body in her car in a parking lot. They said she'd taken too many pills, and her heart just stopped beating.

"Dad came back just long enough for the funeral. I begged him to take me with him, but he said his new wife didn't want any more children; she already had three of her own.

"When Dad turned me down, I realized he didn't love me at all. And I felt Mom didn't either. I pleaded with her to quit taking those pills, but she took them anyway, and died and left me. I had aunts and uncles, but they all hated me too. I begged every one of them to take me, but they let me go to foster care instead. So I decided to quit asking anybody for anything. I decided I'd just be quiet and let the world wonder what I was thinking. And I decided I'd never trust anyone, ever again.

"You and Julie and Mr. Greene have been so kind to me," Melinda continued through her tears, "that I

can't help myself. I don't *want* to trust you, but everything in me does."

The mother-heart in Mrs. Greene was weeping for this lost young girl. Drawing Melinda into her arms, she silently embraced her for a long time. "You did the right thing to tell me, Melinda," she finally said. "No one should have to face such a hurt alone.

"But one thing I can tell you for sure: God brought you here to our home. *He* loves you very much. He loved you when your mother died; He loved you when your father and your family rejected you. He loves you now, and He wants to take that hurt from you. Jesus will never fail you. Do you want to put your trust in Him?"

Melinda nodded, and Mrs. Greene carefully and simply explained the plan of salvation.

"Dear Jesus," Melinda prayed without prompting, "Please forgive me for not trusting You. I come to You now and ask You to cleanse my sins with your Blood and receive me as your child. I trust You now. Amen."

At that moment, a sleepy-eyed Julie appeared, looking for her weekend roommate. The new Julie was introduced to the new Melinda, and the angels rejoiced in heaven with the happy trio on earth.

19

The Return Of Mad Michael Murdock

With the entrance of Melinda into the family of God, the sisterhood of the four friends was now complete. The girls not only had the armor of God with which to face the problems of public school, but they had each other in a new way. Lunchtime at Pleasant Hope High School became their oasis in the middle of the desert.

While other students were discussing the next school dance, the four girls would be sharing their burdens with one another in prayer. They never made a show of this, but everybody knew what they were doing.

One day in the cafeteria, Julie looked up to see Mad Michael Murdock suddenly appear at the end of the long table. He nodded his head in Julie's direction, and just in case that nod was really meant for her, she smiled back sweetly. Julie learned that Michael was registering as a new student that day – and once again, he showed up in her English class.

Mrs. Kent offered Michael a seat in the back, or the empty one behind Julie. Without a hint of recognition, Michael chose the seat behind her.

Julie didn't press her luck by trying to speak to Michael, and her patience paid off. That very day, Mrs. Kent introduced her plan for a unique writing

assignment. "Each student in the class will pair off with the person behind him or her and you will interview each other. Then with that information, you will write a short biographical sketch about your partner for your homework assignment tonight."

The whole class expressed their displeasure with grunts and groans, but Julie smiled to herself as she recognized God's hand in this assignment. With a brief silent prayer for wisdom, Julie turned around to face a highly uncomfortable Michael Murdock.

Mrs. Kent had mentioned no specific questions they should ask each other, so Julie took the initiative, hoping to break the ice which was rapidly forming a glacier on the desk between them.

"Well, Michael, I haven't seen you since the sixth grade. Where have you been keeping yourself?" She hoped a little lighthearted warmth would help melt the iceberg.

"My dad is a career officer in the Marines," Michael answered with obvious pride. "Our family spent the last four years in Japan." Julie tried not to let the shock register on her face. She would have been less surprised if Michael had announced that his father had been in prison.

Relieved that her first question had been such a hit, Julie continued with more confidence. "Did you learn any Japanese?" she asked with undisguised curiosity.

"Nope," Michael answered. "We pretty much stayed on the base and went to school with the other Marine brats."

Well, that question was a dud, Julie thought to herself, pleading with God for another opening. "How about doing our interviews this way," Julie suggested. "I've asked you two questions; now you ask me two. Otherwise we may not get through both interviews before the bell rings."

"Why did you help me in the sixth grade when I cut my wrist?" Michael blurted out without hesitation.

Ignoring the fact that this question was not typical for an interview, Julie answered him simply. "Because you needed help. The year before your accident, someone helped me in a similar way, and I've never forgotten it." Then she found herself telling Michael the whole story of the creek incident, including her own bad behavior.

Michael sat up from his usual slouch and listened intently to Julie's story. It was a new experience for him to hear anyone talk with such honesty. When she was through, he had a second question. "Do you mind if I write the story in the interview?"

Oh no, Julie said to herself. *I forgot this could all end up in the interview.* She had wanted to leave her life in Baysville buried forever. But she also remembered her choice made at Thanksgiving years ago – to live a life of open gratitude to Jesus no matter what it cost her. She answered with sure conviction, "Whatever you write about me, Michael, will be just fine."

Julie and Michael both got so involved in getting acquainted that they forgot to take notes. When the bell rang, they realized they would have to trust their memories.

But whatever the outcome, Julie knew that it had been a worthwhile experience. She felt that God had turned an enemy into a friend, and that was something to shout about.

The next day, Mrs. Kent called on Julie to read her interview first. "I thought you might all enjoy hearing about Michael," the teacher explained, "since he is new to our class."

Some of the kids who remembered Michael from elementary school sneered silently. Julie completely ignored their snide expressions and began to read her paper.

"Yesterday I interviewed Michael Stephen Murdock Junior. Michael was named for his father, who is Colonel Michael Stephen Murdock Senior, United States Marine Corps." Julie looked out at her open-mouthed audience with amusement. Resisting the urge to say, "And now that I have your attention," she continued reading her interview.

The class listened as Julie reinterpreted the boy formerly known as Mad Michael. They heard, among other things, that Michael had lived four years in Japan, that he liked football, and that he enjoyed asking his classmates difficult interview questions. The class laughed at that line, knowing now how hard it could be on either side of an interview.

"Thank you, Julie," Mrs. Kent said with a smile. "Now, I know the rest of the class would like to hear what difficult questions Michael asked you. So we'll have him read his interview next."

"Yeah!" the class chimed in jovially. Michael rose to his feet, looking embarrassed. He was used to receiving negative attention, but he did not know how to handle positive reception.

He cleared his throat and began, "Julie Greene is a very unusual person. She doesn't like to talk about herself; she's more interested in other people. I knew Julie from a distance in elementary school. I was one bad dude, as some of you recall." (Several snickers from the classroom.) "When I cut my wrist in the cafeteria, Julie stepped forward to help me, when no one else did. That's the kind of person she is, in a nutshell. I'm glad I got to interview her."

Not a word of the creek incident was mentioned in Michael's interview. Although the students were a little embarrassed by Michael's honesty about himself, they all gained a new respect for him that day.

But both Julie's and Michael's interviews had given the rest of the class something to think about, which would not soon be forgotten.

20

I Can Say No

Julie had so many things to think about these days that her mind was continually in a dither. One major focus was Melinda. She knew from experience how important fellowship is for new Christians, and she tried to think of ways she could help Melinda in her walk with the Lord. She had already been amazed at how quickly Melinda was growing on her own.

The Sunday morning following Melinda's experience with Jesus, she voluntarily stood up in church and shared it with the entire congregation. That night, Julie rode along as Mr. Greene took Melinda home. They went as far as the door together, then Julie paused as Melinda suddenly ran into her foster mother's arms.

"Mrs. Carver," she cried, "I've only been thinking of myself all these years. You've done your best with me. Will you forgive me?"

Not only was Mrs. Carver shocked to hear three complete sentences roll off Melinda's tongue, but the sudden expression of gratitude was almost more than she could take. She hugged Melinda right back, and suddenly the roles were reversed. Mrs. Carver could not think of a single word to say!

At that point, Julie quietly backed out and closed the door. Such a moment should not be broken with a mere hello from her. The memory of that encounter still brought Julie joy every time she thought about it.

Another focus of Julie's thinking was Michael Murdock – no longer Mad Michael, but a new friend. Every day, she sought to nurture their friendship in a way that would draw him toward Jesus.

But Julie's most pressing concern was another choice that lay just ahead. She had been surprised and delighted to get a solo in the spring choir concert, but later dismayed when she read the lyrics of the number Mr. Frazier had chosen. This year's selection was from the Broadway musical *Oklahoma*, by Rodgers and Hammerstein, and Julie's solo was a song called *I Can't Say No*. Julie was not so sheltered as to miss the implication of what the song said.

Fortunately, Mr. Frazier had announced his choice for the solo casually, in front of the entire choir. Julie would have time to consult her parents regarding the best way to handle the situation. But deep inside, she had already made the decision to refuse the part.

That afternoon, Julie got off the bus with a heavy heart. Never was she gladder to know that her mother would be waiting for her in the house. Mrs. Greene's cheery "hello" melted into sober concern when she saw Julie's face. "What's the matter, Julie?" asked her mother with heartfelt sympathy.

Julie was crying as she shared the whole problem with her mother. She explained that she had already made the choice to refuse the solo, but the hard part was how to tell Mr. Frazier. She loved her teacher, and

did not want to offend this kind man – who would not
be likely to understand or appreciate her choice.

"We'll talk about it tonight when your father gets
home, Julie. I'm not sure what the best approach is.
Maybe Dad will have an idea. Meanwhile, dry your
tears. I do know that it pleases God when we trust
Him even *before* we get his answer to any problem."

That night, Mr. Greene listened to the dilemma,
and offered his advice. "If I were Mr. Frazier, I'd just
appreciate the simple truth. Why don't you go see him
after school tomorrow and tell him how you feel?"

Julie instantly knew in her spirit that this was
God's answer to the problem, and she was able to set
aside the issue for tonight with quiet confidence

The next afternoon, Julie approached Mr.
Frazier's office with fearful steps. She found the
teacher sitting at his desk. "Excuse me, Mr. Frazier,"
Julie said softly. "May I speak with you a moment?"

"Of course, Julie. Please have a seat."

Julie was glad to sit down. It made it easier to
resist the temptation to run away. Her heart beating
fast, she took the plunge. "Mr. Frazier, I'm so honored
that you chose me for a solo, but I can't in good
conscience sing that selection. So I'll just have to opt
out. I hope that doesn't put you in a bad position."

Mr. Frazier's eyes were red, but not from
emotion. He had been an alcoholic for many years,
but was able to keep his position because he was
talented enough to do the job whether sober or not. He
had been choir director at Pleasant Hope High School

for over twenty years, and he was universally loved both by his students and the community.

"Thank you for coming in, Julie," Mr. Frazier responded hoarsely. "I'm glad you told me how you feel."

Sensing that his remark signaled the end of the conversation, Julie rose to leave. The choir director turned his attention back to the sheet music on his desk.

Though the encounter was brief – even terse – Julie felt good about it, and told her parents so when she got home.

The next day, at choir time, Mr. Frazier made an announcement. "We will not be using the selection *I Can't Say No* in our *Oklahoma* medley for the concert. I believe it is inappropriate." That was all. Every eye was on Julie, expecting her to be disappointed and wondering what on earth she was smiling about.

Julie went home that day with a song in her heart. It only had four little words: *I CAN say no!*

21

Sisters Twice

The days rolled into weeks, the weeks into months, and all of a sudden, senior year arrived for Julie and her friends. The girls walked down the senior hall on that crisp autumn morning, before the bell rang to signal the beginning of the first day of school.

College boards, career choices, and financial decisions loomed ahead of them, but none of these challenges dampened the party atmosphere among the seniors that day. Today they were finally going to enjoy "senior privileges," like all the upper classmen had done before them. This tradition went back as far as any teacher could remember.

Freshmen, sophomores, and juniors had to wait for the first bell outside the walls of the building. Seniors alone had the privilege of coming inside and visiting with each other before school. That privilege meant even more when it was raining, or when the cold wind whipped through the parking lot.

But that was not all. At lunch time, seniors were always served first in the cafeteria line, no matter when they arrived. Lower-classmen took all this in good humor, knowing that their turn would come someday.

Julie, Jennie, Melinda, and Cecelia – along with a few other girls who had attached themselves to the group – took full advantage of the before-school privilege to visit with one another. Even Michael Murdock occasionally joined them in conversation, though he was still pretty much of a loner.

About three weeks into the school year, something happened to Julie and Melinda that would change their relationship in a permanent way. While the girls were in school, Mrs. Carver came over to see Mrs. Greene. Sweetly declining the usual coffee, she went right to her errand. It was a matter of great importance, and she needed to get it off her chest.

"I just found out this morning that my mother is extremely ill and in need of full-time care. I feel that my place is with her. The problem is, Mother lives far away, and I'm not in a position to take Melinda with me. I know that this is asking a great deal, and I will not blame you if you turn me down, but you and your family love Melinda so much, and she loves you. I wonder if there's any way...."

"Mrs. Carver," Mrs. Greene gently interrupted, "We do love Melinda – like a daughter. She already spends so much time here that it would seem natural for her to move in permanently. I can't give you a final 'yes' until I talk it over with my husband and Julie, but I'm just sure they'll be as thrilled as I am at the possibility. I'll call you tonight with our final answer. In the meantime, you might see what you can work out with Melinda's social worker."

Mrs. Carver was overcome with relief. She and Melinda had finally established a bond between themselves these last two years, and the dilemma

about leaving her behind was now one of love rather
than obligation.

"We won't have to deal with the social worker,"
noted Mrs. Carver, returning to practical matters.
"Melinda will turn eighteen the first week of October.
She will be in a legal position to make her own
choices."

"I don't suppose you've spoken to Melinda about
this yet," Mrs. Greene wondered aloud.

"No, I wanted to check with your family first. I
thought it might make the news of my leaving easier to
take. She's lost so many people in her life already.
You'll never know how much this means to me,"
added Mrs. Carver tearfully.

"I'm so glad we can be of help," answered Mrs.
Greene. "God has really changed our family from
what we used to be."

Mrs. Carver had already been an eyewitness to
that transformation, as she had seen its fruit in
Melinda's life. A seed had been planted in her heart
which would undoubtedly be watered in the years to
come.

Now it was Mrs. Greene who could not wait to
see Julie emerge from the school bus that afternoon.
Upon hearing the news, Julie could not contain her joy
– and did not try to. Not knowing how else to express
it, she threw her arms around her mother and hugged
her so tight that her mother jokingly called for oxygen.

That weekend was both joyous and sad. The
Greenes had invited both Mrs. Carver and her foster
daughter to Sunday dinner. Mrs. Carver had even

gone to the worship service with Melinda that
morning. She was scheduled to leave for her mother's
home the next day.

Saturday had been well spent moving Melinda's
things into the Greenes' house. It was then that
Melinda shared with the family her divided feelings.
She had truly grown to love her foster mother and
would miss her terribly, but she was also grateful and
thrilled to become a permanent part of the Greene
household.

"Hey," Julie remarked that Sunday. "Now we're
sisters twice!" Even Mrs. Carver understood the
implication, and smiled knowingly

Melinda had already spent so many hours in the
Greene home over the last two years, that this year as a
real member of the family was like one long weekend.
The only difference was that now she was a real
daughter, not a guest.

Both Mr. and Mrs. Greene, as well as Julie, were
obviously grateful and pleased to have Melinda with
them, and Melinda could feel their unconditional love.
At her birthday dinner two weeks later, she received
two gifts. One was from Mr. and Mrs. Greene, and the
other was from Julie. It was signed, *Your sister, twice,
Julie.*

The gifts were beautiful – a matching gold
bracelet and necklace – but the best gift of all was a
new set of parents who loved her, and a sister she
could call her very own.

"Thanks, Mom. Thanks Dad. Thanks, Sis."
Melinda's eyes glistened with emotion and excitement

as she said each name. And with that short speech began a natural transition into her life as Melinda Greene.

22

Graduation Countdown

Senior year whizzed by more quickly than ever as Julie and her friends approached graduation day. Mornings now in senior hall were hectic with animated conversation. The high school prom, two weeks away, was the primary topic – but none of the four girls had any interest in the event.

Antioch Church was offering an alternate celebration for high school seniors from their church, and any senior classmates they wished to invite. The four friends looked forward to a special dinner prepared by some of the best cooks in Brighton – Antioch's senior citizens. After that, they were set to enjoy whatever surprise agenda the old folks could invent. It should be an interesting evening.

Julie herself had even more cause to celebrate. Ted, who was completing his freshman year at Ashburn Teachers' College, had accepted her invitation to Brighton for the event. He also promised to bring Big Jake, who had enlisted in the Marines and was scheduled to ship out in a few weeks.

When Ted wrote Julie to accept the invitation, he alluded to some other important news that he thought best to tell her in person. Julie supposed that Ted might be making plans for the ministry, but she let the subject go at that. She had so many other things to think about.

One of the hardest "no's" Julie had ever had to say was to Michael Murdock, who had finally summoned up the courage to ask her to the prom.

He had caught her by surprise in the hallway during senior morning time. In her mind, Julie played back her response over and over again. She knew the Holy Spirit must have inspired her with the words to say, as they seemed to have the right effect on her friend.

"Michael," she had answered, "let me say to begin with that this is the nicest invitation I have ever had; it was so thoughtful of you to ask me. But I feel like I need to share some things with you.

"I'm not a fan of rock and roll music, and I don't dance. I also don't date. That was originally my parents' decision, but they left it up to me once I turned eighteen, and I agree with their perspective. Marriage is probably a long way in my future – after college at least – so I don't see any point in dating now, if it isn't going to lead to anything. In any case, I think group gatherings are both safer and a lot more fun.

"I've invited several of my friends to Antioch Church for a special senior celebration. It's going to be held the same night as the prom. Michael, I would be so honored if *you* would come to *our* party."

He smiled sheepishly. "I can't say I'm not disappointed, but I respect your decision. That's the thing I really like about you, Julie – you live what you believe."

Michael left her with a promise to consider her invitation. As he walked off, he added with a grin, "I can't dance anyway."

As Julie watched her friend disappear down the hall, she silently praised the Lord. She recalled a Scripture verse she had memorized the week before: "It shall be given you in that same hour what ye shall speak...."

The weekend of the senior dinner, Julie was invited to stay at Jennie's house, along with Cecelia and Melinda. Jennie's brother was away at college, so they had plenty of room. The Greenes, meantime, prepared a guest room for Ted and Big Jake.

Expecting the boys to arrive around noon on Saturday, Julie and her friends drove over early so they could be there to greet them. Instead, *they* were greeted by two surprises. The first was that Ted and Jake had arrived early, having left Baysville at four o'clock in the morning. The second shocked Julie to the core, for when she saw Ted and Jake sitting in the living room, she saw not one uniform, but *two*.

The boys stood to their feet respectfully when the girls came into the room. A torrent of thoughts rushed through Julie's mind, but by God's grace, she was able to keep her own counsel for the present. "Well, two eyes," she said lightly, "you've really gone and done it now." Then Julie turned to introduce them to her two friends and her new sister.

The rest of the morning passed quickly, as everyone tried not to talk at once in getting acquainted and sharing their news. Julie and Ted went out on the back porch after an hour or so, anxious to have a private conversation.

"Why?" Julie asked her friend simply, the tears brimming over in her questioning brown eyes.

"Julie, the week before I was to leave for second semester at Ashburn, I was reading from the third chapter of Proverbs. When I came to verse six, I knew suddenly that the Lord was speaking to my heart. That verse says, 'In all thy ways acknowledge Him, and He shall direct thy paths.'

"I realized then that I had moved ahead of the Lord in going on to college. It had just seemed like the next natural step at the time. I decided to wait on God and not to move ahead until I was certain of his will.

"Then I learned that Big Jake was enlisting, and I somehow knew that God wanted me to join with him. Because we both signed up instead of waiting to be drafted, we were eligible for the 'buddy system,' which means we can stay together wherever we are assigned. I am convinced that God is in this, Julie, so whatever it means, I'm in his hands."

Julie knew that she too needed to leave Ted in God's hands. She made the choice to trust God without understanding all the "why's," and the peace that passes understanding flooded her soul.

Ted and Julie went back into the house to join the others for lunch and fellowship. About 3:30 Mr. Greene offered a very important reminder. "The dinner is at six tonight. Don't you girls have some dressing up to do?"

Simultaneously, Julie and Melinda looked at their identical Christmas watches and gasped. "We'll see you later, guys." Then the girls piled into the car and headed back to Jennie's house to get ready for the evening. Though sobered by Ted's announcement, Julie found herself willing and able to enter in to the spirit of celebration for the evening.

23

A Time To Laugh

Julie had a strong heart – which was a good thing, because another shock was waiting at Antioch Church that evening. There in the parking lot, looking starched and stuffed into an obviously new suit, stood Michael Murdock. Trying to hide their surprise, Julie and the other girls went right over and welcomed him warmly.

With Michael being the only male in the group at this moment, the girls were afraid he might change his mind and make a panicked getaway. But just then, Ted and Jake arrived. Their presence – and their blue dress Marine uniforms – put Michael at ease immediately.

The seven young people walked over toward the fellowship hall, wondering what the older generation had in store for them. As they neared the door, where several other teenagers were waiting patiently, a wonderful aroma permeated their nostrils. An intelligent guess told them that someone was grilling steaks. (Actually, one would have to be a complete dodo not to see smoke coming around the corner of the building.)

The door to the fellowship hall was shut, with a humorous note taped to the door. "Patience Is a Virtue!"

Soon enough the door was opened, and the entire group was awed at the scene which awaited them inside.

The first thing they noticed was a hand-lettered banner hanging on the back wall. Most of the young people recognized the Scripture they had learned as a song in vacation Bible school. "HE BROUGHT ME TO HIS BANQUETING TABLE, AND HIS BANNER OVER ME IS LOVE!"

Tables had been placed end-to-end and covered with a lovely white cloth. Each place setting had a napkin rolled into the shape of a diploma, and tied with a golden tassel. Little graduation caps, carefully printed with names, served as individual place cards for each graduating senior. Invited friends could choose any place to sit where the mortarboard read *Special Guest*.

At the piano in the far end of the fellowship hall sat 93-year-old Mr. Maupin. With no sheet music in sight, he was unobtrusively playing a medley of lovely Gospel songs.

Julie was amazed. She knew that Mr. Maupin was a faithful member of the flock at Antioch, and that he was a retired engineer, but she had no idea he could play the piano. Mrs. Watson, the hostess, told the guests that Mr. Maupin had actually been a concert pianist many years ago.

A delicious salad adorned every plate as the guests found their designated seats. Each stood behind his chair as pastor Steve stepped up to offer a blessing.

Then they all sat down to a meal that would last a lifetime in their memories.

After rib-eye steaks, baked potatoes, and homemade crescent rolls, the teenagers were asked to move to the U-shaped arrangement of chairs at the far end of the hall. There they visited while a volunteer crew of young people cleared the tables and relieved the worn-out kitchen committee in doing the dishes.

Thirty minutes later the clatter of plates and glasses ceased, and Mrs. Watson announced that they were ready to begin the rest of the festivities.

"Since all of you will soon be graduating from high school, we old folks thought it might be fun to see how much you've learned. As it happens, there are seven girls and seven boys here tonight. So if you gentlemen will arrange the chairs in two rows facing each other, about ten feet apart, we will begin the first competition. Boys on my left and girls on my right.

"I believe one of the courses you study as seniors is public speaking. I have in my hand a canning jar with a number of useless topics chosen by our committee. The object of the game is to see how many points your team can accrue by speaking extemporaneously on a topic you choose from the jar. You will receive one point for every minute your teammate is able to keep speaking, without straying from the chosen topic.

"Hopefully, we will have one volunteer from each team. Otherwise we'll have to draw straws."

Getting into the spirit of the game, both teams began discussing among themselves who would be the best choice to represent them. "Any volunteers?" asked Jennie pleadingly. From the last seat in the row, a timid hand was raised. Was there to be no limit to surprises this evening?

"Are you sure you heard the question, Melinda?" Cecelia inquired incredulously.

Melinda just nodded in good-natured humor.

"Okay," Jennie said. "Our team is ready, Mrs. Watson."

From the other side of the room, Big Jake volunteered for the boys' team. "We're ready too," shouted the boys together, as if a football game were about to begin.

First up was Big Jake. Everyone laughed as he tried to extract his huge hand from the mason jar. Then he opened the little folded piece of paper and read his subject aloud. "Lemon rinds." He was given ten seconds to get his thoughts together, and then had to begin – ready or not.

"Lemon rinds has always been a subject near and dear to my heart. I have wanted to give a talk on lemon rinds ever since I was a little boy and I am truly honored, extremely pleased, and elated today to have the opportunity to pursue this topic which is of great interest to me and I'm sure to you who cannot wait to find out what I could possibly say about a subject so obscure, so petty, so trivial, so boring, as lemon rinds." On and on he continued, as both sides roared with hilarity.

After Jake had accrued four points for the boys' team, he ran out of senseless drivel. To the accompaniment of appreciative applause on both sides of the aisle, he bowed three times and returned to his seat.

Rising bravely to the occasion, Melinda gingerly reached inside the canning jar. Looking perplexed, she read the topic aloud: "Cold remedies." Without hesitation, she jumped right in. "The best remedy for the cold is heat." Missing entirely the obvious reference to the common cold, Melinda continued along this line. The rest of the crowd found her misinterpretation quite comical, and listened with amusement as she described every way she could think of to obtain heat.

Melinda might not have been able to speak about cold remedies for very long, but when it came to heat sources, she could have gone on for hours. (She had been awarded the Science Prize for graduating seniors the week before.) Realizing that they might be there all night, the group finally applauded her off the stage after she surpassed Big Jake's four points.

The performance was not only fun, but also a glory to God. All who knew what God had done in Melinda's life, rejoiced at the obvious transformation.

Once again, Mrs. Watson came up to announce the winner of the game – the girls. Then she turned and uncovered a blackboard that had been concealed with a white sheet. "Welcome to Christian Jeopardy," she quipped. "But, instead of answering with a question, we made questions for you to answer." She read the topics aloud across the board – history and geography, spelling, music, math, and Bible.

"The losing team from the first game will have first choice of categories. Pastor Steve will serve as the master of ceremonies, assisted by Mr. Maupin."

Michael Murdock was suddenly grinning so widely that Julie could count his teeth across the room. In a little huddle with his cohorts, he whispered something to the rest of the guys and they all yelled "GO!" Then they smugly chose to begin with the Spelling category.

"Spelling for one point," announced the emcee. "Spell *extemporaneous*."

Michael immediately jumped to his feet – the signal in this game to express one's readiness to answer. The girls giggled, but went silent as Michael spelled the word without hesitation: E-X-T-E-M-P-O-R-A-N-E-O-U-S. Football cheers rang out from the boys' side of the room. They all knew something the girls didn't: Michael was a natural-born speller. The only A he made in elementary school was in spelling – and he rarely had to study.

Needless to say, the boys dominated that category handily with a total of fifteen points. "Since the boys seemed to hog that category, girls," said Pastor Steve, "I'm going to exert pastor's privilege and let you choose the second one."

There was no need for deliberation among the girls. Five of them were members of Antioch Church, and well acquainted with the Word of God. "Bible!" they chorused with glee.

The first question was pretty obvious. Ted managed to stand a second faster than Julie and grabbed the one-pointer: "What book of the Bible has the most chapters and how many chapters does it have?"

"Psalms, and it has a hundred and fifty chapters," answered Ted triumphantly. Question number five in the Bible category was a real doozy: "Name at least one of the daughters of Zelophehad." Jennie jumped up immediately, but she needn't have hurried. No one else on either team had a clue.

"Is it okay to sing the answer?" she asked.

"Sure," agreed Pastor Steve curiously.

Clearing her throat, Jennie sang Numbers 36:11 to a bouncy little tune: "For Mahlah, Tirzah, and Hoglah, and Milcah, and Noah, the daughters of Zelophehad, were married unto their father's brothers' sons."

"Very good, Jennie!" exclaimed the pastor. "Where did you get that song?"

"My mother made up Scripture songs for me when I was little," Jennie explained. "This one was just to show that you could sing *any* Scripture and remember it. I just about drove her crazy singing it over and over!"

By the time the game was over, the participants had learned some interesting facts about one another. It turned out that Sam Atkinson, the star quarterback of the football team, knew more than how to make a pigskin fly. He also knew the capital of Ghana.

In Music for one point, Mr. Maupin played few notes on the piano and asked if anyone could name the composer.

"Tchaikovsky," Julie answered confidently.

Without breaking rhythm, Michael immediately stood up and spelled *Tchaikovsky*. Once again the fellowship hall echoed with healthy laughter.

The last question, designated on the blackboard only as "Final Mystery Question," was also under Music. Mr. Maupin began the opening notes on the piano, and all at once Ted, Jake, *and* Michael stood up to attention. Speaking for the other two boys, Michael answered, "That's the Marine Hymn."

When the game was over, the boys had a clear win. But by then, no one seemed to care. It had been a special moment for these three guests in particular, as well as for those who had invited them.

"Now," announced Mrs. Watson, "you young folks may rest your voices a minute, so the Antioch Gospel Quartet can sing for you and still make their nine o'clock curfew. As everyone knows, we old people go to bed with the chickens and get up with the sun."

While the kids had another good laugh, four old men shuffled out on stage. One of them had a pitch pipe, and with it signaled the beginning note of a rousing Gospel song, *Rock Me, Lord*. The music echoed through the fellowship hall in ancient, yet sweet and powerful harmony.

"Encore!" shouted the audience as they applauded.

The lead singer gave a signal to the other three, and they worshipfully began their favorite selection, *He Touched Me*. On the second verse, Mrs. Watson waved a hand toward the young people, inviting them to join in.

Julie's eyes once again filled with tears as she added her voice to this testimony in song. *"Since I met this blessed Savior, since He cleansed and made me whole, I will never cease to praise Him, I'll shout it while eternity rolls."* If ever a song expressed how she felt about the Lord, this was it.

The moment was too holy for applause. Ted stood to his feet, and said, "I know that I'm just a guest here, but I want to say that your singing really ministered to my spirit tonight. Thank you. And I believe I speak for all of us, in thanking you for an absolutely scrumptious meal as well as the unique entertainment and games." A round of applause then erupted for the senior citizens of Antioch Church.

Meanwhile, the younger people had reset the dinner table with homemade apple pie and ice cream. The graduates and guests spent the rest of the evening enjoying dessert and coffee, and mingling with their friends.

The whole evening was perfect, a memory to last forever. And Julie knew that she could be a part of it only because Jesus *had* reached down and touched her, right where she was, in the icy waters of the creek so many years ago.

24

Two Steps Forward

As the girls pulled out of the parking lot that night, Julie looked back and saw Ted, Jake, and Michael leaning against Michael's car, engrossed in serious conversation. Julie prayed that it would be fruitful.

Sunday morning dawned too quickly for the girls, who had stayed up in their own after-party talk until past midnight. Willfully they dragged themselves out of bed and got ready for church.

From her spot in the choir loft, Julie was thrilled to see that Michael had come with Ted and Jake. Pastor Steve preached an anointed sermon on the Second Coming of the Lord. He called for a period of silent meditation at the close, and invited anyone to step forward who had questions or was ready to surrender his life to Jesus Christ.

Jake was sitting on the aisle seat, and Michael was sitting next to Jake. Both boys stood up at the same moment, and walked solemnly in step down to the front together.

According to the pastor, Michael had questions and asked for prayer. Jake's questions were already answered, and he was ready to give his heart to Jesus. As Ted sat in the audience that morning and watched his best friend become his brother, tears of joy streamed freely down his face.

Julie rejoiced as much for Ted as for Jake. After the service, she invited all three of the boys to lunch. Cecelia and Jennie were coming too. It would be their last opportunity for fellowship before the boys had to leave. Ted and Jake were scheduled to report to the Marine base that evening to await deployment, and they had a long drive ahead of them.

The Greenes' small house was bursting at the seams for Sunday lunch. Mrs. Greene decided to have cold cuts, to give the young people more time to visit before they had to leave.

Julie and Ted agreed to keep writing while he was overseas, but phone calls would of course have to be set aside. Melinda, Jennie, and Cecelia all promised to write both boys, which helped to sweeten their departure. Michael also promised to keep in touch with his two new friends.

When Mr. Greene realized that the time was at hand to say goodbye, he took charge to smooth out a moment that might otherwise have been awkward. Taking his wife's hand on one side and Ted's on the other, he suggested that they form a circle and pray for the two new soldiers. All those gathered joined hands and approached the throne of an ever-watchful Father.

The boys then grabbed their duffel bags and, with a hasty goodbye, took to the road. After all their friends had gone, Melinda went upstairs to unpack.

Julie followed her mother to the kitchen to help clean up. As she did so, she suddenly began to cry, and grabbed her mother for physical support. With her mother holding her, she wept it all out.

Then, just as suddenly, Julie became sober. "I'm okay now Mom," she said. "God loves Ted more than I do, and I have no right to want anything for him other than God's perfect will. I know that the song is true that says 'Jesus doeth all things well.' At least, I know it in my head – now I'll have to learn it with my heart.

25

Letting Go

Julie had originally chosen Ashburn Teachers' College because that was where Ted had enrolled. He had given her glowing reports about the Christian atmosphere there, as well as the English curriculum – but what she had really looked forward to was going to school with him again.

Because of this, Ted's unexpected decision to join the Marines was doubly hard on Julie. She tried to keep giving the relationship back to God, but the cold, hard facts were beginning to crowd her spirit and destroy her peace. Not only would she be without Ted's presence at college, she would also have to trust God with the perilous situation overseas.

Julie needed more help with this problem than any she had ever faced. It seemed more than she could bear, and all her efforts to keep a "stiff upper lip" proved temporary. Finally, she went to see Pastor Steve.

"Come in, Julie," said her pastor warmly when he answered her knock at his office door. "We haven't had a chance to chat since the weekend of the senior party. Those were two nice young servicemen you invited. I had a good talk with Jake after the service, and I believe he means business with God."

"Ted is a wonderful Christian, Pastor Steve, and he's had a special burden about Jake for a number of

years. They're the best of friends, and I'm so glad for
both of them. But I really came here to talk about a
personal problem.

"Ted and I have known each other for eight years,
and I think what I feel for him is something more than
friendship. His going overseas has really thrown me
for a loop. I just can't seem to reconcile myself to our
being separated, even though I know he's where God
wants him. I've yielded to the situation at least ten
times, but I just can't seem to keep the victory. I know
I should have lasting peace about it, but I don't."

"Perhaps that's because you're only yielding to
the situation," suggested Pastor Steve, "instead of to
the Lord Himself. Julie, what if God showed you that
his plan for your life would not include Ted – ever?
Could you reconcile yourself to that?"

"I guess I'm not sure," Julie answered
uncomfortably.

"You need to relinquish Ted and your future
together into the hands of God," advised the pastor.
"The Lord wants nothing less than total yieldedness
from his children. Jesus told us that we must love Him
more than our families, and even our own lives, in
order to be his disciples.

"Julie, I think you have a room in your heart
where you keep your love for Ted, and the plans you
have involving him. And on the door of that room,
there is a sign that says "Off Limits." You'll never
have peace until you take that sign down and yield
every aspect of your life to Jesus."

Although Julie knew that pastor Steve was right, she felt resistance to his answer. Thanking him weakly for his advice, she took leave to consult with herself.

That evening, as Julie paced her room and struggled with the question, she was reminded of the first time her dad had told her *no* about something she wanted very badly.

Julie knew that it would only make her miserable to resist God's will. Falling on her knees by her bedside, she yielded that last room of her heart to the sovereign will of her Father.

Suddenly that indescribable peace returned, flooding Julie from head to toe. With a heart of thanksgiving, she rose from her knees – cleansed, forgiven and filled anew.

Julie was surprised at the grace she felt to face attending Ashburn without her dearest friend. Perhaps it was because she had learned that there was a Dearer Friend to her than Ted.

Shortly after Julie shared with the family what the Lord had done in her heart, Melinda approached her sister with an idea.

"Julie, maybe the Lord wants the two of us to be together in college. I'm sure the elementary education department at Ashburn will have the classes I need. I know it's late in the year to be changing schools, but if Ashburn will accept my application now, we could take that as confirmation from the Lord that this is his idea and not just mine."

Julie was overwhelmed by Melinda's offer. She noticed most what Melinda did not suggest – that Julie could change her own college plans to be with *her*. How she loved her sister, and her Lord.

And so it was that the Greenes drove both daughters to Ashburn Teachers' College that fall. By the end of the first semester, Julie realized how much she had needed the time to get to know Melinda better. The year they had spent under the same roof had been their senior year in high school – a time awhirl with activity and changes.

Both of the girls' freshman roommates at Ashburn dropped out after one semester, and so they were able to room together for the rest of the year. Spending every evening with Melinda now, Julie began to notice that she had an eager pen pal of her own – Jake.

Both Jake and Ted wrote to the girls that God was moving powerfully in their unit, and confirming their decision to volunteer for overseas duty. Already, Ted reported, six of his buddies had given their lives to Jesus.

Julie and Melinda, in turn, shared the spiritual victories they were experiencing on the home front. Instead of feeling the sense of separation she had feared, Julie increasingly felt spiritual oneness with Ted – as well as with Jake and Melinda – in living life one day at a time, walking in the steps of Jesus. By sharing their burdens with each other, they multiplied the number of prayer warriors available for battle, whether in Vietnam or at Ashburn Teachers' College.

Sometimes the battles came in unexpected places. One of them was Ashburn's required freshman Bible course, the one class Julie and Melinda shared.

Their first semester, covering the New Testament, was wonderful. It was taught by Dr. Williams, and felt more like church than a college class. The professor, a former atheist, set the tone on the very first day by sharing his personal testimony. Honestly (but without unedifying detail) he communicated how he had been the chief of sinners, and how God had marvelously brought him into the light. His openness made the students respect him immediately, and his teaching was simply anointed.

Second semester, the girls were scheduled to take a course in Old Testament, but they found that Mr. Brown opened his class on an entirely different note. "There are many lessons to be learned from the fine old stories in the Bible," he told them in the first lecture, "but that's just what they are – stories. In this class, you will learn practical applications, which hopefully will enhance your moral character."

"Did I just hear what I think I heard?" Melinda whispered to Julie as they walked back to the dorm.

"I hope we misunderstood him," Julie answered. "Maybe he didn't mean it exactly as it sounded. Let's just wait and see."

The girls did not have to wait long. In the second session, Mr. Brown taught on the story of Moses and the Red Sea. He explained his theory that the part of the sea where the Israelites crossed over was merely marshland, and that the division of the waters was only

figurative. He then went on to expound the "moral" of
the story, as if it were one of Aesop's Fables.

Julie and Melinda had no idea what to do. That
night in the dorm they read from James 1 to encourage
one another: "If any of you lack wisdom, let him ask
of God, that giveth to all men liberally, and upbraideth
not; and it shall be given him."

"Lord," Julie prayed, "we need your wisdom now
for this situation... Oh!" she suddenly interrupted
herself as a light came on. "Melinda, quick, where's
your curriculum guide?"

"On the shelf," Melinda replied curiously.
"Why?"

Julie flipped through the booklet, then pointed
triumphantly to what she was looking for.

"I can't believe we didn't think of this before,"
the girls said together.

Before they call, I will answer.

The next morning, Julie and Melinda went to the
registrar's office and asked to switch to Basic Hebrew
– the one course that could be substituted for Old
Testament on the college's curriculum schedule.

The girls did not realize that the man standing
behind them was Dr. Harman, president of the college.
"Excuse me, ladies," he interrupted. "Just being nosy.
Is there a problem with Mr. Brown's class?"

Their hearts visibly pumping in their throats, the
girls explained the situation.

The president looked astonished. "No student
has ever told me about this," he said. "You are quite

right to take this step, and I will look into the matter personally."

That night, Julie and Melinda devoted their prayer time to praise and thanksgiving. They were learning by experience the security of being thrust on God alone.

26

"God Leads His Dear Children Along"

One evening in their dorm room, Julie and Melinda were taking a break from studying. Julie started quietly singing her favorite chorus, *Only Believe*, and Melinda joined her in a soft alto. They were singing to the Lord alone, but someone else happened to be listening as well. Caroline, their suite-mate, had just turned off the water in the adjoining bathroom. She tapped on their door and then cracked it open. "Nope," she commented lightly, "it's not angels."

Inviting herself in, Caroline plopped on the bed and asked for an encore. Julie and Melinda obliged with another gospel song they both loved, *Until Then*.

Before they knew it, Caroline was joining them every night for worship, and what started as three quickly grew into a body of twelve believers, meeting there in the dorm.

Not all of the other students appreciated the small group's overt devotion to the Lord. It was one thing to go to a Christian school and maintain the traditions of one's denomination. But all this bubbly enthusiasm about Jesus was just embarrassing. For this reason, many of them simply avoided the girls and their friends.

Others, like Sharon Smith, were more vocal in their objections. Julie and her friends would be standing together in the cafeteria line, and Sharon would yell out some rude remark. "Well, just look at the assembly line of praying hands!"

Julie and her friends were so joyful in the Lord, they barely noticed the mocking and snubbing. In fact, Julie was amazed to find herself reluctant to leave for the summer. Just nine months earlier, she hadn't been sure she could even *come* here without Ted.

Julie and Melinda did look forward to one thing about summer vacation: Jake and Ted would be ending their tour of duty in Vietnam, and would be home on leave the whole month of August. The four had made plans to spend some of that time together in Brighton.

When August finally arrived, the girls had already been home for a month, during which they had enjoyed plenty of quality time with their family, church, and old friends like Jennie, Cecelia, and Michael.

Michael, who had burst an eardrum in a freak accident when he was four, was designated 4-F by the military. Staying in touch with Ted and Jake gave him some sense of participation in the war, but he still felt a bit guilty remaining in college while his buddies were risking their lives overseas.

Although outnumbered by his female companions, Michael gravitated to spending time with them over the summer months anyway. He had given his life to Jesus that spring, and found that Christian fellowship always lifted his spirits.

The five were gathered at Julie's house, packing a picnic basket, when there was a knock at the door. Julie's heart skipped a beat. In her spirit, she sensed something was wrong.

Opening the door, she saw Big Jake standing there – all alone. Not a word was spoken. The deep hurt in Jake's eyes told the whole story. Julie threw her arms around his huge neck and wept silently. She'd often imagined such a scenario, and had thought that her heart would break physically in half if it happened.

But looking around her, Julie realized that she was not the only one in need of solace. She and her precious friends must now find their comfort in the Lord together.

Slowly Jake came into the house, his arm still around Julie's shoulders. The group sat down in the living room and waited while Jake began to unfold the details of Ted's death.

"Both Ted and I were scheduled to finsh our tour of duty in just two days," Jake began. "The truck was supposed to pick us up that afternoon. We were on patrol in the jungle, when a group of snipers opened up on us from the surrounding trees. One of our buddies, Cliff Gray, was pinned down in the clearing, severely wounded and unable to move."

His voice breaking, Jake finished the story quickly. Ted had rushed to Cliff's side and dragged him to safety in the bush. A single shot to the head and Ted was gone – but not before he had saved his friend.

Julie was both devastated and yet strangely peaceful. Months ago she had yielded to God's will, whatever it might be, and she would not start questioning now.

Early the next morning, a solemn caravan began their sad trek back to Baysville to witness the closure of Ted's journey on earth. Jake and Michael rode together, while Julie and Melinda followed with Mr. and Mrs. Greene.

Jake invited Michael to spend the night with him at his parents' home. Julie had called the Gladstones ahead of time, and Mrs. Gladstone had insisted that the Greenes spend the night with them.

"Rebecca and Sarah are away as camp counselors this week," she told them, "so we have two spare bedrooms – enough for you, Melinda, and your parents."

The moment Julie walked into the peaceful Gladstone home, she was glad her family had accepted the invitation.

David and Ruth served as ministering angels, strengthening the entire Greene family for this difficult time. The two families communed far into the night, and their wise counsel helped Julie to see this present valley more from God's perspective.

There were many tears that evening, but also unexpected laughter. The families enjoyed comparing notes of their recollections from opposite sides of the neighborhood fence.

Julie had never heard the story of how Rebecca found her doll the first day they "met." And the

Gladstones had never gotten the scoop on what
happened to Julie after she got home. Julie laughed
harder than anybody else about how God had *caught*
her in the act.

They talked with the Gladstones until two in the
morning, and went to bed truly comforted. This
family, who had shown them the true meaning of love
so long ago, was still showing it today.

The military funeral was scheduled for the next
afternoon. Jake and Michael took Julie over to the
Carrolls' house an hour before the service.

Ted's mother looked pale but lovely as she
answered the front door. "I'm glad you're here, Julie,"
she said as they embraced. "I have something for
you."

Leading Julie to Ted's room, Mrs. Carroll opened
his top dresser drawer and withdrew a long, slender
box with a letter taped to the outside. "I found this
when I was going through his things," she explained.
"The envelope is addressed to you."

Handing Julie the box, Mrs. Carroll quietly left
the room and closed the door behind her. Julie's hands
trembled as she carefully unfolded the note inside the
envelope, and began to read through her tears.

"My dearest friend, if you are receiving this
letter, then I am already in the presence of Jesus. I
hope that the grief of this temporary separation will
turn into joy as you continue your own journey with
the Lord.

"I believe our hearts were knit together as one the
day we ran into each other in the library, spilling all

those books. It was God's plan all along to call me
home early. Trust Him, Julie. He loves you more than
I ever could.

"In the box is our seashell. It may not have any
ridges left, I've taken it out so many times. You'll find
a jade ring in the box as well, just about the size of
your little finger. The glowing green color reminded
me of you. The circle represents eternity, because
that's how long our friendship will last. Just as the
seashell was a memento of our childhood, please take
the ring to remind you of what awaits us as children in
the kingdom of God.

"His alone, Ted."

The rest of the day was a blur to Julie. She had
left that room without shedding any more tears,
mindful that Ted's parents might need her calm.

The military ceremony was dignified, respectful,
and beautiful. Ted's pastor, at the request of his
parents, had preached a simple sermon: *Jesus Christ,
The Only Way*. Ted's younger sister, Susan, had sung
her brother's favorite hymn, *God Leads Us Along*. The
first verse goes like this:

> *In shady green pastures so*
> *   rich and so sweet*
> *God leads His dear children along*
> *Where the water's cool flow*
> *   bathes the weary ones' feet*
> *God leads His dear children along*
> *Some through the water,*
> *   some through the flood*

Some through the fire,
  but all through the Blood
Some through great sorrow,
  but God gives a song
In the night season,
  and all the day long

Julie had never heard that song before, and it touched her spirit like nothing else in the service. As the gathering of believers left the church single file for the graveyard located immediately behind, Julie could still hear the words echoing in her mind. "Some through great sorrow, but God gives a song...."

The military escort performed the traditional 21-gun salute, and presented Mrs. Carroll with the American flag that draped the casket.

The service had been perfect. Adjusting to life without Ted would be another matter, for all of them.

27

Sunshine And The Seashell

At this point in the story, Grandma Greene began staring out the front window, lost in a moment of reverie. Suddenly, she was drawn back to the present, as Donnie was giving the hem of her outer shirt an urgent tug.

"Grandma," he said with concern, "Emily's crying." Suddenly, it dawned on Grandma what had happened. She had carelessly mentioned the jade ring. Suggesting to the children that they play outside for a while, Grandma gently led Emily back to her bedroom.

"Emily, I'm so sorry to have mentioned the ring without talking to you first. I had completely forgotten about what you shared with me, until I saw you crying."

"Oh, Grandma, I didn't know that *you* were Julie." Emily reached into her pocket and took out the little jade ring. "I brought this back today to give to you. Now that I know what the ring means, it hurts all over again that I could have done such a thing."

"Emily, remember what I said a minute ago? I told you that I had completely forgotten about the incident. God has forgotten too. He says in his Word that He has removed our sins 'as far as the east is from the west.' You mustn't grieve over this. Jesus already bore all our griefs."

"Thank you, Grandma. I *am* different since I told you what I did, and I want to stay that way. Here's your ring."

Grandma returned the ring to her jewelry box, then pulled out something else, brought it back, and placed it in Emily's hand. Emily gasped. It was the seashell.

"Emily, I feel like the Lord wants you to have this. You already know the story behind it. Now you can continue your own story with the seashell in your possession. Who knows what experiences await you and your seashell in life."

Emily threw her arms around Grandma Greene's ample waist. "Oh, thank you, Grandma. I'll treasure this all the days of my life."

"Let it remind you, Emily, that the true treasures are the eternal ones – just like the circle of Ted's ring. You're part of that circle too. I love you, and you are one of my dearest treasures.

"Let's keep this conversation our little secret for now. No one else seems to have caught on as to who Julie is, and there may be more surprises in store for the rest of the club. Now let's go out to the kitchen and make some lemonade to go with the animal cookies we're having for snack."

It was such a lovely day that Grandma thought it wise to save the rest of the story for another Saturday. She sat out on the deck in her two-seater swing and watched the children playing croquet – all except Donnie. He was entertaining himself with a bottle of bubbles Liza had found for him in the toy chest.

Grandma observed the children with gratitude in her heart, knowing that her times with them were part of the joy and fulfillment God had planned for her life. It was a privilege just to follow the Bridegroom who had laid down His life for her.

The children had a wonderful time that afternoon, and when Grandma called them in, there was barely time for a "lick and a promise" before their parents would arrive.

Donnie was proud of his new job and did it as faithfully as a miniature soldier. When Grandma completed the countdown, Donnie turned his attention to the club members and began his count. "One – two – three – four – five – six – seven," he carefully numbered. "Grandma, I thought you said there were eight of us with Charlie here today. I only count seven."

Liza scooped up her favorite toddler and pointed to the mirror on the wall. "There's number eight!" Donnie laughed at himself gleefully, and they all laughed with him.

It had been a good day, and the children were sorry to say goodbye. Charlie was as much of a little gentleman as his friend Tommy, and thanked Grandma Greene for letting him stay. He asked if he could come again, and Grandma assured him that she would miss him if he didn't.

Every day in the Lord is good, mused Grandma, as she waved goodbye to her precious children.

28

Peaches, Pears And Other Fruits

"Peaches, pears, and paper towels are on the kitchen table," announced Grandma as the Saturday Only Club members arrived that morning. (She mashed a banana in a bowl for Donnie, as bananas were the only fruit he liked. Besides, she was not interested in giving a three-year-old a bath this morning. The other kids were messy enough.)

Grandma began to stoke the fire in the living room, while listening to the sounds of squishing and slurping as the children noisily consumed their morning snack. Charlie and Tommy followed her.

"Grandma," said Tommy, "Charlie and I had a late breakfast this morning, so we're saving our fruits for after lunch. We'd like to tell you something while we wait for the others to finish, if that's okay."

"I'm all ears," chuckled Grandma.

"Well," Tommy began, "after you told us the story of Julie when she was a backyard bully, Charlie and I started thinking. There's a boy in our class who sounds just like that, but he looks more like the way you described Mad Michael Murdock.

"Our teacher, Mrs. Justice, didn't realize how Josh was acting out on the playground. Just like Julie, he knew how to behave in the classroom, when he wanted to. We didn't want to get him in trouble, so we decided to do what Genevieve did when she offered Julie her blue shovel."

"A week ago," chimed in Charlie, "Tommy brought his football to school, so he and I could play catch at recess. The very first time we passed the ball, Josh intercepted it and ran off laughing and tossing it in the air to himself. He only threw it back once the bell rang for the end of recess. He did the same thing the next day, and the day after that."

"So," added Tommy, "yesterday, we pulled a 'Genevieve' on him, and threw a pass *to him* at the beginning of recess. Boy, did that throw Josh! He almost dropped the ball, he was so surprised."

"Then," Charlie added, "Tommy yelled to him across the yard, 'Nice one!' Josh threw the football back to Tommy, and started to walk away. But Tommy yelled, 'Josh!' and threw him another high pass."

"That was some recess!" finished Tommy with a grin. "It's just like you told us, Grandma – now our enemy has become our friend."

Tommy and Charlie hadn't noticed the rest of the club gathered just outside the living room, listening curiously. But the eavesdroppers had gotten an earful, and neither of the boys seemed to mind.

"Thanks for sharing, boys," said Grandma as she noticed the others standing there. "True stories are the best stories, and we all needed to hear that one."

Seeing fruit pits and cores still in sticky palms, Grandma instructed, "Now, half of you line up at the kitchen sink, and the others go down the hall to the bathroom sink. We'll resume our story in five minutes, ready or not."

Five minutes later, the club took their places once again in the living room, and Grandma picked up where she had left off in the life of Julie Greene.

"The new school year at Ashburn Teachers' College could not start soon enough for Julie. She would be glad to be busy again. Melinda was not quite so eager, as she was finding Jake's company most agreeable. However, she made no mention of this to Julie. Melinda was devoted to her sister, and always tried to consider Julie's feelings above her own."

College prayer group was still intact when the girls returned that fall. Mindful of Julie's recent loss, the other girls were supportive in every way possible.

The circle of friends was serious about their study of the Bible, and especially about prayer. They did not look on it as a religious obligation or a spiritual discipline; they saw prayer as a means to an end. They prayed about everything, and God answered about everything. It was just as simple as that.

One night Julie was awakened by a vigorous shake to her shoulder. The lights were off in the dorm, and no one was supposed be out of their room at that hour. Too groggy to be afraid, Julie slowly recognized Sharon's face as the other girl shone a flashlight toward herself.

Sharon motioned her to follow into the bathroom. Then she flipped on the light and poured out her

problem to the very person she had ridiculed last
spring.

"It's my fiance, John," Sharon told her anxiously.
"I just got off the phone with him, and I'm afraid he's
going to do something to himself. The college has
suspended him for a semester, and he's sick about the
thought he might be drafted. He told me he'd rather
kill himself and get it over with. And then he just
hung up."

Sharon burst into tears at this point. Julie did the
only thing she knew to do: She knelt down with her
hands clasped, leaning on the tub. Julie felt strangely
confident that God would answer this prayer – even
more so, when Sharon scooted up beside her with her
own head bowed.

"Father, we are totally helpless," Julie began with
fervor. "We don't know what to do, but our eyes are
upon You. You have all power. You made John. You
know everything about him. Please intervene in the
situation. Please spare his life, Lord. He's not ready
to die. And Lord, while you're at it, please use this
situation to show Sharon that she needs a Savior too.
In Jesus' Name, Amen."

As it turned out, Sharon's concern about John had
been fully justified. That same night, just before bed,
John's mother had decided to check and make sure his
space heater was off. In the dim glow of the night
light, she suddenly noticed the open bottle of her
tranquilizers on the table by the too-still form of her
son. She quickly called an ambulance, and the tragedy
was averted. But that wasn't the end of the story.

In the hospital, the night nurse assigned to watch John just happened to be a Christian. She shared her personal testimony with her patient – how the Lord had delivered her from a life of alcohol and depression, and had given her a new start.

Right then and there, Sharon's fiance prayed to receive Jesus. He told her about it on the phone the next day, and finished by saying, "Sharon, you need to meet Jesus too."

The day following, Sharon once again saw "the assembly line of praying hands" in the cafeteria. This time she did not shout. She ran right up to Julie and gave her a hug that almost made her spill the tray.

Nobody remembered what they had for lunch that day, but they all enjoyed a feast of good news as they rejoiced with Sharon – who now was more than ready to hear what they had to share with her.

29

A Box Of Tissues And The Touch Of God

In Julie's senior year, she had to do eight weeks of student teaching at a local high school in order to finish her degree. Being under no illusions as to what public schools had become, Julie approached this assignment with fear and trembling.

Providentially, Julie's supervising teacher was also a Christian, and conveniently ignored some of the strange things Julie said and did in the classroom.

During the 1960's, prayer and the reading of Scripture were legally ousted from public schools. In lieu of more obvious opportunities for a witness, Julie decided to put up a famous quote each day on the blackboard, and assign her students to write down what they thought about it.

Beginning with the famous sayings of Abraham Lincoln and Benjamin Franklin, Julie finally worked her way around to using one of the Proverbs of Solomon. Approaching the Bible from a literary perspective was still acceptable in public schools, and thus Julie was able to feed her students with thoughts from the Word of God.

> *Better is a dinner of herbs where*
> *love is, than a stalled ox and*

> *hatred therewith –*
> *– Solomon*

As Julie was adding the last flourish to this quote on the blackboard, Quinton – "the question man," as he was nicknamed by his fellow students – immediately raised his hand.

"Miss Greene," he said. "Who is Solomon?"

The fish had taken the bait, and Julie began to reel in her catch. "Solomon was king of Israel, and was considered to be the wisest man that ever lived. He was also one of the major writers in the Old Testament portion of the Bible. He lived around 1000 B.C.

"By the way, can anyone tell me what B.C. and A.D. stand for?"

Several hands went up immediately. Julie called on Chuck, who knew that B.C. meant "before Christ," but thought that A.D. stood for "after death."

"You're on the right track, Chuck," Julie answered. "B.C. does stand for before Christ. A.D. stands for *Anno Domini* which is Latin for *in the year of our Lord*. It is historically interesting that even the timeline of the modern world is based on the birth of Jesus Christ.

"Now, you have five minutes to write your thoughts about this quote," Julie added casually. Turning to the blackboard she said to herself, "Score one for the Lord."

Julie loved her student teaching experience. She made a point of learning all her students' names within the first few days, not only so they would know that she cared about each of them, but so she could picture their faces as she prayed for them.

She taught five classes with about 25 students in each class. That gave her 125 souls to whom she could be a living testimony. That opportunity far outweighed even the tremendous fun she had in teaching.

After student teaching was completed, graduation once again was on the horizon. Melinda had already signed a contract to teach at Baysville Elementary, the school Julie had attended as a child. Julie followed suit and signed up to teach in Baysville as well, so that once again the girls could room together as they entered the professional world.

Jake came down from Baysville to help them move. It was becoming obvious that he and Melinda were more than just pen pals. Why else would she choose Baysville to begin her teaching career?

Jake was enrolled as a day student at a state college only twenty miles away. He had always enjoyed coaching the little guys in basketball during the summer, and felt like the Lord might have something for him to do along those lines. But with a double major in physical education and business administration, he felt he would be well prepared for whatever God had in mind.

Julie was assigned to teach eighth grade English at Baysville High School. She was grateful not to be at the elementary school, where many of the teachers still remembered her from the bad old days. Mrs.

Peach was still going strong in the first grade, and often interacted with Melinda. One day Melinda discovered a bit of information about the teacher that Julie had never known. "Her name," Melinda told her sister solemnly, "is Georgia."

Julie stared back at her. "Georgia... Peach?" Then they burst out laughing. Georgia Peach described her perfectly – and it was her married name!

The sisters decided to attend Pastor Goodman's church, the one where Julie and her parents had been saved. Pastor Goodman was aging, but his care for the flock had not waned a bit. It made the girls feel more secure, being away from their parents, to have this fatherly man available for counsel.

Time passed quickly as both Julie and Melinda tried to make the classroom not just a place of education, but a haven where children would feel wanted and loved. Some of their students felt neither wanted nor loved in their own homes, and Julie and Melinda had a number of opportunities to apply their Christianity in practical ways.

Julie's heart was touched by one particular child in a way she never forgot. Diane was an eighth grader, both unkempt and uncomely – and only passing English because Julie graded her on effort rather than progress.

One day Diane came to school with a terrible cold, and sat miserably in the back of class without even the comfort of a box of tissues. Julie went over to her desk, and handing her a full box of Kleenex, spoke quietly in her ear, "Diane, why don't you go on home? You really need to be in bed."

"Ain't got a phone," she rasped, coughing. "Ain't got nobody to take me home."

Julie's heart was bursting with compassion, as she said to Diane, "I'll take you home right after this class. I have a free period at that time."

On the way to the girl's house, Julie stopped at the grocery store and bought a gallon of orange juice, several cans of chicken soup, and a box of honey-and-lemon cough drops.

When Diane opened the door of the rundown apartment where she lived, Julie immediately spied a young woman passed out on the couch, with an empty liquor bottle still in her hand. Not wanting to intrude on the scene or embarrass Diane, Julie handed the grocery bag to her student and backed out of the doorway. "Hope you feel better, Diane. Please try to get some rest. Just remember that Jesus cares."

Julie returned to school with a greater appreciation for her own home and upbringing – and with gratitude that Jesus had given her the privilege of expressing his love to another lost lamb. With a prayer that this small act of kindness would bear fruit for his glory, Julie returned to her classroom in a state of sober reflection.

The fruit had ripened by Christmas time. The last day before Christmas vacation, Julie found an unusual gift waiting for her on the teacher's desk. Although the giver was anonymous, Julie recognized the tissue

box that Diane had used in creating a handmade diorama of the manger scene.

Not only was Julie touched by the significance of the scene laboriously created in the little box, but she knew just how much Diane had loved that box of tissues. She had kept it on her desk at school for weeks, sharing it with any student who asked, and offering it to any nearby who needed a tissue but wouldn't ask.

Julie was learning that God could take the smallest things and touch a heart for eternity. She knew that both Diane and she would never be the same, all because of the touch of the Heavenly Father on their lives that day.

30
Melinda's Choice

Julie and Melinda had been teaching a full three years in Baysville, and had begun a fourth, when Jake and Melinda finally announced their engagement. Julie immediately began looking for another roommate, since the couple was planning to be married in June, following Jake's college graduation.

But October brought an unexpected crisis. As children the girls had celebrated Halloween, and to their knowledge, Pastor Steve had never addressed the subject at Antioch Church. But one Sunday in September, Pastor Goodman mentioned it in his sermon, and what he said was not positive. "Halloween is a celebration of darkness," the pastor explained, "with evil roots and connotations. The Lord has shown me that I should no longer condone it, and I would encourage each of you to seek Him regarding your own participation."

The pastor's message resonated with both Melinda and Julie; they themselves had never been fully comfortable with Halloween. But as teachers in a public school, they knew what a stand on the subject could mean. Nonetheless, they decided to make it. Julie had it easier, since high school students had no special activities related to Halloween. Melinda taught a third-grade class, and knew that her choice might be a costly one.

Having shared the problem with the prayer group at church, the girls waited for wisdom from the Lord as to what to do. Melinda did not have long to wait.

"Teacher," said Johnny on Monday morning, "My mommie says to tell you that she will be glad to help with the Halloween party this year. She has this really scary witch's costume she wants to wear, and she says she'll bake all kinds of black and orange Halloween cookies."

"Johnny, please tell your mother thank-you for her offer, but I don't plan to have a Halloween party in our classroom this year."

Johnny's face fell as he returned to his seat, and Melinda knew that this would not be the last she would hear about the subject.

After lunch recess that day, her classroom was as still as a morgue. Even her problem child, Celeste, stayed in her seat and drew Halloween pictures in lieu of her usual attention-getting antics.

"Lord Jesus," Melinda prayed silently, "give me your strength, and help me to respond with love in this situation." The afternoon dragged on. The silence was broken only by the bell, signaling the end of school.

As the children filed dejectedly out, Melinda busied herself cleaning the blackboard. "Goodbye Miss Greene," called out little Lily. "I don't like Halloween anyway," she added more softly. "It scares me."

Melinda's resolve was strengthened by that one remark. If she could protect even one child from the negative effects of Halloween, she would consider herself happy. But whether or not she saw any fruit from her choice, she knew that her place was on the Lord's side no matter what.

That night was hard for Melinda, even with the prayer and support of Jake and Julie. She had not felt such heaviness and dread since that night so many years ago when her mother didn't come home, and nothing her friends could say or do seemed to lift her spirit.

Finally Jake sat down beside his bride-to-be. "Melinda, after Ted died, I felt lower than low for weeks. Even when you and I were out having fun together that summer, I couldn't stop thinking about him – and all the other friends of mine who didn't come back. I started having dreams about them, and also dreaming that other friends died. I was getting depressed and anxious, and I couldn't sleep.

"Then God showed me what to do. The problem was, I was focused on myself and my grief and my fears, and they just made me sink lower. But Jesus said He would take that 'spirit of heaviness' and give a 'garment of praise' instead.

"I know we're facing what could be a devastating situation, and praising the Lord is the last thing you feel like doing, but I'm telling you, it's the only thing that can lift you up. And it's not something we can do for you."

Melinda looked lovingly into Jake's eyes, and then into the eyes of her sister. Then she too made the thanksgiving choice she had heard Julie mention so many times. "I'm thankful for you, Jake," she began. "And you, Julie, and Mom and Dad, and our friends. And I'm thankful most of all that Jesus is strong when I'm weak, and that He's promised never to leave us."

As Melinda continued thanking the Lord for everything she could think of, her spirit was gradually lifted above the worries of that night. The confidence of the Lord replaced her despair, and the three of them were able to enjoy the evening together.

Melinda was summoned to the principal's office first thing the next morning, but she went with calm assurance not of her own making.

"Miss Greene," began the principal abruptly, "I had a call from Johnny Powell's mother yesterday afternoon. Do I understand correctly that you told Johnny that there would be no Halloween party this year in your classroom?"

"Yes sir, Mr. Nelson. That is true. Hosting such a party conflicts with my Christian convictions about Halloween. I cannot in good conscience participate any longer in that holiday celebration."

"There *will* be a Halloween party in your classroom, Miss Greene. Whether you attend or not is entirely up to you. I will get a substitute teacher for that day if you so desire. Please let me know your decision by the end of the week."

As principal of the elementary school, Mr. Nelson had been primarily responsible for hiring Melinda in the first place. They had always enjoyed a good working relationship. But now he stood with his hand resolutely on the doorknob, his body language

signaling the end of the interview – and his deep
displeasure with the third-grade teacher.

Melinda's knees were shaking, but her spirit was
strong. As she walked back to her classroom, she kept
on remembering Who was walking beside her.

Melinda did not feel peaceful about the idea of a
substitute teacher. It would avert the crisis and relieve
her of responsibility, but it might also muddle her
witness to the children.

"I know it sounds extreme," she told Jake and
Julie that evening, "but I believe the Lord wants me to
resign. I cannot hide from this issue and keep a clear
conscience. I want to be able to tell my class why I
am leaving. I think I should tender my resignation
immediately, and offer to stay until they can find a
suitable replacement."

"I'm with you," Jake agreed readily.

"It's a scary step to take," added Julie honestly.
"But like the Bible says, we have to obey God rather
than man. I really don't feel like we have any other
choice."

Melinda smiled at Julie's use of the term *we*. It
was comforting to know that Julie would stand behind
her no matter what.

There were practical matters to consider.
Melinda would be without an income; she and Jake
had based their wedding plans on being able to
purchase a house. Jake had not yet graduated, nor did
he have a position lined up for the next year. They
would all just have to walk by faith and let God write
the story.

The next day, Melinda told her class that she was leaving and why. Though some were still miffed about the Halloween party, none of them wanted to lose Miss Greene as a teacher.

After explaining about Halloween she added, "I have enjoyed being your teacher these last two months. You're a good class, and I'll miss you. I hope you realize that what I'm doing is out of concern for you, as well as obedience to God."

Melinda had placed her resignation in the principal's mailbox. He asked to see her at lunch time. "I regret to see you taking this step, Miss Greene," he said. "I hope you won't be sorry later on."

"Mr. Nelson," answered Melinda, looking her principal in the eye, "when it comes to a choice between pleasing people or pleasing God, I must choose God. I'm sure He has a plan for my life elsewhere. Thank you for giving me the opportunity to teach these last three years."

She smiled warmly at him and returned to her classroom with victory in her heart. Mr. Nelson shut the door to his office, having second thoughts. He hoped that *he* would not be the one to be sorry later.

Melinda had the joy of seeing several positive results of her choice before her final day at Baysville Elementary. She was not the only one absent from class the day of the Halloween party. Lily's mother had kept her home, and three other students were also mysteriously missing that day.

From students who *had* attended, Melinda learned that Johnny's mother had made her appearance at the party, but the response to her witch's costume was generally one of indifference or aversion. Most interesting of all, Mrs. Peach had taken personal leave on the day of the party as well.

Mr. Nelson wasted no time in finding a replacement for Melinda. The story was making its way through the community with mixed reviews. By Thanksgiving, Melinda had fulfilled her obligation to the school. She drove home with assurance in her heart that God had been glorified in this trial, and would faithfully see her through the future.

31

The Two-Room Schoolhouse

Baysville Christian Academy got wind of Melinda's resignation and contacted her after the Thanksgiving holiday. Mrs. Miller, their first-grade teacher, was expecting a baby in the beginning of January, and needed a substitute for the following six weeks. Melinda got off the phone with the principal of the Academy, but Julie had to put it back in the cradle herself. Melinda was shaking with sheer amazement at what God had done, and in such a timely fashion.

Following this temporary teaching assignment, Melinda found herself substituting at Christian Academy almost every day. She had quickly earned a reputation for being reliable and responsible.

Julie made it through the end of the first semester that year without any major problems. She did notice that the other teachers eyed her more distantly, probably because she was Melinda's sister. But Julie took that in stride; it came with the territory, when you lived what you believed.

Over the welcome break of Christmas, the girls went home to Brighton. Jake drove them down so that he could spend part of the holiday with Melinda and her family. Melinda's foster mother, Mrs. Carver, was also in town for a short visit, and Melinda wanted Jake to meet her.

That Christmas was not only a season of happy reunions, but also of new possibilities. Antioch Church in the last few years had experienced physical expansion as well as spiritual growth. With the increasing number of families in the fellowship, they had begun to consider the possibility of starting a Christian school to accommodate their children.

Mr. and Mrs. Greene had been giving the church continual updates on Julie and Melinda in the last three years, so they were all aware of Melinda's resignation over Halloween. After much prayerful consideration, a church committee approached all three young people with a proposal. They wanted to start an elementary school – with Julie as principal and Melinda as teacher for girls. Jake could teach the boys, and would also direct physical education.

"And I could help with reading, composition, and music!" Julie enthused, embarrassed by her display of zeal, but too excited to hold it back.

The committee cautioned that pay would be minimal starting out, but promised to provide a house for Jake. After some fixing up, it would be suitable for the soon-to-be Robinson family. Until then, they all knew the Greenes would be more than glad to have the girls back home.

Plans began to move forward that spring. After wrapping up her last long-term substitute assignment at Christian Academy, Melinda returned to Brighton and threw herself into the task of helping to prepare the new school. Jake followed after his graduation, moving into the house provided by Antioch, which was located just across the street. In view of all the repairs and preparation needed for both the house and school, Jake and Melinda decided to postpone their wedding plans until things were well underway in the fall.

Once Julie had completed her own teaching responsibilities at Baysville, she tendered her resignation and eagerly joined her sister in Brighton. That summer was the busiest, happiest time any of them could remember, as they worked together with church volunteers to get Antioch School ready by fall. They cleaned, remodeled, and painted the building. They scoured school sales and auctions for desks and books. And they constantly dreamed up new ideas for biblically-based lesson plans. It was all so exciting, they would have had trouble sleeping if they hadn't been so wonderfully tired at the end of each busy day.

The long-anticipated first morning of school finally arrived. Twenty pairs of squeaky new shoes lined up outside the freshly-painted schoolhouse, as twenty children waited anxiously for the ringing of the brass bell. None of them had been allowed to so much as look inside the school building yet, and all were bursting with anticipation. They would not be disappointed.

Finally the new principal emerged and rang the school bell with fervor. Julie greeted each child by name as they filed into the schoolhouse. Parents stood along the walls, not wanting to miss a minute of this brand-new educational beginning for their children.

Before the boys and girls were led to their separate rooms, Julie asked Pastor Steve to offer a blessing on their school. Tears of gratitude were abundant as both parents and children realized what an opportunity the Lord had given them.

Trying not to run, the boys then followed Mr. Robinson into their classroom. The girls, conscious of being ladylike, meekly followed their own teacher. *Oohs* and *ahs* echoed in the hallway as the children discovered all the surprises awaiting them.

Each had his own desk, with school supplies stacked on top of it. Both rooms were decorated with brightly-colored bulletin boards and welcome signs. But what was most exciting was the atmosphere. There was no underlying feeling of pressure and tension such as public school students endure. Antioch School didn't really feel like school at all. It felt like *home*.

The opening of school was such a success that it was difficult to get the parents to leave so the day could start. Julie tactfully invited them into the office area, where she answered questions and filled them in on the still-developing curriculum.

As fall progressed, more ideas were introduced for the benefit of the children. When the church decided to add a Bible course, Julie jumped at the chance to teach it. To her, it wasn't additional work; it was more like heaven on earth.

After the struggles in public school, it was indescribably wonderful to be able to exalt the Name of Jesus openly, and to teach every course from a biblical perspective. All three teachers felt more like they were playing school than teaching it. Julie, in particular, knew that this was what she was born to do.

32
"O Perfect Love"

It was time for Thanksgiving again, in more ways than one. Jake and Melinda had chosen the last week in November for their long-delayed wedding, as things were beginning to settle down a bit, and the house was nearly ready. The timing couldn't have been more appropriate. In the year since Melinda had made her choice to obey God rather than men, all of them had been blessed beyond their wildest imagination.

The ceremony took place at Antioch Church, and all the old gang participated. Jennie, still unmarried, served as an attendant to the bride, as did Cecelia – now Mrs. Michael Murdock. Cecelia's young husband, the newly appointed Assistant District Attorney, was a groomsman. Sharon and several of the girls from college were bridesmaids. Even Sarah and Rebecca Gladstone showed up in the audience to surprise Julie and Melinda, and brought a special friend they knew that Julie would be delighted to see.

Most poignantly, Jake's best man was none other than Cliff Gray, the soldier whose life Ted had saved at the cost of his own. Cliff was now a Christian, and happily married with his own family.

Mr. Greene had never felt so happy and proud as when he walked his lovely daughter down the aisle that day. Who would ever guess that this beautiful and confident young woman was the silent and rejected

"Mouse" of many years ago? But then again, she really wasn't – nor was Julie, nor were any of them. *If any man be in Christ, he is a new creature. Old things are passed away; behold, all things are become new.*

As Jake and Melinda joined hands before the pastor to give their heartfelt vows, Julie sang from the choir loft. The selection was a wedding hymn called *O Perfect Love:*

> *O perfect Love, all human*
> > *thought transcending,*
> *Lowly we kneel in prayer*
> > *Before Thy throne,*
> *That theirs may be the love which*
> > *knows no ending,*
> *Whom Thou forevermore dost*
> > *join in one.*
>
> *O perfect Life, be Thou their*
> > *full assurance,*
> *Of tender charity and*
> > *steadfast faith,*
> *Of patient hope and quiet,*
> > *brave endurance,*
> *With childlike trust that fears*
> > *nor pain nor death.*
>
> *Grant them the joy which*
> > *brightens earthly sorrow;*
> *Grant them the peace which*
> > *calms all earthly strife,*

And to life's day the glorious
unknown morrow
That dawns upon eternal
love and life.

Julie had once imagined that she and Ted would have this day, and that Melinda would be the one singing *O Perfect Love* as Ted slipped the ring on her finger. But Julie now had another ring, the jade ring that symbolized eternity. Unconsciously she fingered it now, thinking of the day when she would once again see her dearest friend, and they would never more part. Until then, her life was full – just as God had planned it. She might never know the love of a husband, but she certainly knew the love of a Father, and she had the privilege of giving that love to his little ones.

Julie was content.

33

Surprise Party

"So Julie never married?" Liza asked as Grandma finished the story. "That's so sad. I was hoping she'd find someone else."

"Oh, it's not sad at all," Grandma told her glowingly. "Children, Julie had the happiest life you could imagine. She stayed on as principal of Antioch School until just five years ago. During that time she got to touch hundreds of young lives as they passed under her care.

"Melinda soon decided to leave teaching, as she and Jake had several children and she wanted to stay home and raise them. She taught them herself in the early grades. So, like some of you, the Robinson children were 'homeschooled' for the first few years. Then they went on to high school at Antioch – just as you will, Liza, at the new building – where Julie and an ever-increasing staff of teachers helped to guide the rest of their education.

"A long time ago, Julie had a conversation with Mrs. Gladstone about the different callings people have in life. Mrs. Gladstone compared God's plan for each life to a 'recipe.' If we yield to his special recipe for us, the result is happiness and fulfillment. Some of the ingredients may seem bitter in themselves, but the whole will be perfect when finished. However, if we try to follow his recipe for somebody else, we'll be miserable and miss the whole point of life.

"Julie's recipe was to shape and shepherd the children of others. Melinda's was to have and raise her own, and she did – three boys and four girls. They all grew up to love the Lord, and you kids know some of them. Tommy's and Charlie's teacher, Mrs. Justice, is Melinda's oldest daughter. And Kelly, her youngest, is little Donnie's mother."

When Donnie heard his name called, he awoke with a start. The children laughed as much with pleasure at their connections in the Saturday Only Club as they did at Donnie, who hadn't the faintest idea what anyone was talking about.

"Liza," Grandma continued, "your grandmother always called your great-uncle, her only brother, 'Bear,' but his real name was Ted."

Liza's eyes went wide. "Uncle Bear was Julie's best friend who died in the war?"

"Yes he was," answered Grandma. "You should ask your grandmother about him sometime. He was a wonderful young man, and he'll always live in my heart. You see, children, I can say with confidence that Julie's life was happy and fulfilled, because I *am* Julie.

"I began this club many years ago" she continued, "as a ministry to Christian parents. Each of your parents works hard all week either homeschooling or teaching at Antioch. Having you here for part of the day each Saturday gives them a chance to get some things done or just relax. And it gives this gray-haired old lady some time with some very special children.

"On Sundays, my parents and I have a Sunday service for the senior citizens at their retirement home. My own mother and father are now in their late eighties. How much time we have left together on this earth is in God's hands.

"But the good news is that there is no death for the Christian – only a change of location. Ted has already claimed residence in a perfect world that will last forever, where there is no separation, no grief, and no pain. I plan to join him and all the other believers who have gone before, when God calls my name and takes me home too."

The room was silent and thoughtful. Peering out at all the serious expressions, Donnie looked up at Grandma and said, "Church!" At that they all chuckled again.

"By the way," said Emily. "What happened to Genevieve? Didn't you ever see her again?"

Grandma's eyes twinkled merrily as she checked her watch. "I thought you'd never ask!" she said. "And as it happens, the answer should be walking up my driveway just about now."

As if on cue, the doorbell rang, and there stood a plump old lady, glowing like a light bulb. Julie brought her in with a warm hug. "Children, this is Mrs. Pierce, but you already know her as 'Genevieve,' from Julie's – or rather, my – childhood.

"Remember I told you that Sarah and Rebecca brought a special guest to Melinda's wedding?"

"That was me!" explained Genevieve. "As a young woman, I found myself back in Baysville one day, and I decided to go by the old place and see if Julie still lived next door. I met the Gladstones instead, and they were just about to leave for Melinda's wedding. Being young and impulsive, I decided to grab my bags and go with them."

"I don't know when I've been so surprised," Grandma added. "On the very day I was 'losing' my sister, I gained back a friend I never thought I'd see again. We've stayed in touch ever since."

"Grandma Julie brought me to Jesus in the years that followed," Genevieve told them, "and so our friendship has grown and continued deeper and deeper. I live about two hours from here, and we visit each other every now and then. Julie has kept me posted about telling you her story, and she wanted me to come down today so I could meet you all. Actually she's been pestering me to *move* down here with her ever since my dear husband went Home. One of these days I might just take her up on it! I'm not too old for the club, am I?"

"Do you know any stories like Grandma tells?" asked Phoebe and Peter eagerly, for once in total agreement.

"I just might know one or two," Genevieve admitted with a smile.

The afternoon sped by as the children listened to the two ladies tell story after story, until Donnie fell asleep again, and there wasn't even time for "a lick and a promise."

As the parents began to arrive for their children one by one, Liza approached Grandma Greene privately. "Grandma, I'll be thirteen this year, and too old for the Saturday Only Club. Would it be all right if I came anyway to help you with the younger children? I may not need a babysitter, but you've got something that I do need a lot more. Thank you for everything."

Each member of the club left Grandma's house that day with a lot to think about. Their lives would never be the same, having seen Jesus through the story of a former backyard bully who had found forgiveness and complete contentment in His Love.